C000002078

About the Author

Leo Unadike is a writer and author of the new novel *Oja and the Parrot's Curse*. He was born in Nigeria, but moved and settled in the United Kingdom subsequently. He has a BSc (Hons) degree in Biomedical Science from Kingston University, London. He combines work with writing and maintains a healthy mind, body and soul through meditation, gym and sports. A keen animal lover who has an aquarium with pet fish that do not hesitate to remind him that they see, feel, are eager to stay alive and have their unique tacit ways of showing that they are not very different from we humans after all.

Oja and the Parrot's Curse

Leo Unadike

Oja and the Parrot's Curse

Olympia Publishers
London

www.olympiapublishers.com
OLYMPIA PAPERBACK EDITION

A CIP catalogue record for this title is
available from the British Library.

ISBN: 978-1-78830-882-3

This is a work of fiction.
Names, characters, places and incidents originate from the writer's
imagination. Any resemblance to actual persons, living or dead, is
purely coincidental.

First Published in 2021

Olympia Publishers
Tallis House
2 Tallis Street
London
EC4Y 0AB

Printed in Great Britain

Dedication

Dedicated to you; human, the universe sees you and
appreciates that you are here.

Chapter One

Obinna was his name, and he lived in a small village known as *Umuzura*. The dry season had passed, and the withered crops had begun to grow again. It was the season when the birds could be heard at night humming their mysterious songs like lead vocalists in a choir singing to the tune of the rain as it pelted the bamboo rooftops.

He would scoop a handful of nuts which he had roasted earlier with firewood and a metal pan, throw a few in his mouth first and the rest to the birds outside, through the window, and tell himself that it was the payment for their musical entertainment.

He would stay awake through the night for hours until the sounds from the birds stopped. It is all connected, he thought. They have a voice because I have ears.

"These bird's songs will have no meaning if there was nobody to listen to it," he whispered to himself as he walked across his mud hut to turn down the lantern's wick and save some kerosene for the next day.

"I must catch some sleep soon and look my best for the *Udunre* festival tomorrow," he said to himself as he reached underneath his wooden bed for his flute. He whistled while he cleaned the flute and walked towards the window, which he had previously propped open with a bamboo stick.

"It is my turn now to entertain you," he said while

looking through the window at the birds. With his eyes closed and both hands holding the flute, he blew into it, the song:

Our world is our curse, let us live it without remorse
Rivers flowing with gold or rivers flowing with blood,
who knows, maybe
But if I love you and you love me
Let the rivers dry up; we will sail through you will see.

The birds are now asleep, he thought. He could no longer hear their wings rustling among the nearby leaves as he quietly closed the window, put the flute in a small bag which he tied around his waist and walked back to his bed.

The entire night, Obinna found it hard to sleep as his mind was filled with thoughts of the festival the next day. He would wake abruptly with each loud crack of thunder as the rain carried on through the night and wipe the dribble from the corner of his mouth as he could smell the pleasant aroma of rice and stew from the nearby huts.

Well I have not cooked anything for the festival, but I will entertain the guests and the maidens with my flute, he thought, yawned and fell asleep.

*

Obinna woke up to the sound of dogs barking outside. I feel like I have not slept at all, he wondered and realised he had fallen asleep with the flute in the bag still tied around his waist. He jumped up from his bed, propped open his window with the bamboo stick to let in some light and have a look outside.

"Are you the ones who have been disturbing my sleep?" he said smilingly to the dogs running outside his hut. He paused for a while, "Or maybe you have a message for me?" he giggled as he opened the door to go outside and meet the dogs wagging their tails. Initially, he thought that they belonged to his neighbour, a former village wrestler who had retired due to old age but realised when he went outside that they were stray dogs. He gently pulled each of their tails as the villagers believe that if someone brings greetings to you with their hands stretched out, you do not touch them in the leg or head, you hold their hands, so when a dog wags its tail at you in greeting, it wants you to welcome it by holding its tail.

One of the dogs seemed to be particularly more interested in Obinna than the others. It stood very still, looking at him while the rest circled with a trot. The dog started whining, ran towards him, stood on its hind legs and tried to use its front paws to touch his face. Obinna smiled and caressed its back while the dog stared into his eyes as if it wanted to tell him something. It rested its front paws on his shoulders quite close to his neck. After what seemed like a minute, he reached back and removed the dog's paws from his shoulder with both hands and gently placed them on the ground. The dog's attention became focused on the bag around his waist, which had the flute in it, as it sniffed and licked the bag relentlessly.

"You are a very friendly one, aren't you?" he said, as the dog took one last look at the bag and ran off to join the others.

He waved to the dogs as they departed and quickly went

back in to wash his face, place some water in his small bag and get ready. He could already hear the drummers as they marched in line heading towards the village square where the Udunre festival was customarily held once a year to usher in the rainy season and thank the gods for life and death.

The sun had already risen, and outside, he could feel the gentle breeze from the north as it caressed his skin. He would smile each time he thought of it, nod in affirmation and say:

"Yes, I understand." It is all connected, he thought. "You embrace us, we breathe in, and you become us, we breathe out so that you can embrace us again," he whispered to the wind as he took the shorter route to the village square. He would greet everyone he walked past on his way as they were all heading in the same direction.

Obinna suddenly heard footsteps behind him, turned around and saw a very scruffy looking older man. The man's skin was thick and looked as though he had smeared wet charcoal all over himself. The man had a walking stick, a heavy sack on his back and a small empty keg of palm wine tied to his waist and the smell of burnt firewood coming from his torn clothes was quite strong.

"*Dede Nnoo*," he greeted the man in his native Umuzura dialect, "You made me jump; I did not see you were coming," he said.

The man looked at him, and Obinna noticed that a thin white film covered one of his eyeballs and he had a steady gaze.

"We only see what we want to see," the older man replied with a smile.

He must be blind, Obinna thought. "Are you from this Village?" he asked the man, "I have not seen you before."

"I am from *Umunede*," he replied. "I have come for the Udunre festival, to listen to the drums and witness *Udele*, the talking parrot in your village which we have heard stories about from across the hills and valleys."

"Ah, Udele, the talking parrot; she is a mystery that our descendants and we will never fully understand," Obinna replied while walking alongside the stranger. "That parrot is from a long lineage of birds, the first one flew into our village, and our native doctor kept her," he continued, "The native doctor replaces each one that dies with a new bird, but she claims that it is the same soul that lives in all of them." He explained further, "There is even a rumour that the first parrot was once a human who ate a magical fruit, was cursed by the gods and turned into a talking bird."

"We are all cursed," the man asserted while slowly looking up at the sky.

"It is not the curse that matters; what matters is the reason, and how you respond to the curse which then determines the outcome," Obinna explained.

"Sometimes thunder and the great winds strike down old trees, to let new ones grow in its place," the old man said and pointed at the small bag tied around Obinna's waist.

"There is something in that bag, what have you got in there?" he asked, and Obinna replied:

"My flute, it's called *oja*, and I've also got some water." Obinna was concerned, he knew the man must be exhausted as the distance from Umunede to Umuzura was at least twenty miles and he knew that even the young dread the rocky paths that run through the plateau between the two villages.

"Here, have some water and quench your thirst," he said

13

as he patted the man on the shoulder and handed him the water in his bag.

The man quickly grabbed the water without saying a word and began to gulp it down. He paused and looked at Obinna as some of the water trickled down the corners of his mouth.

"It is okay; finish it," Obinna said. "There will be plenty more to eat and drink at the festival."

The man sucked the last drop of water, coughed vigorously and heaved a sigh of relief as he handed the empty bottle back.

"Thanks, you are a good man," he said.

"Let me help you and carry your bag to the village square," Obinna replied as they walked along. "The journey is still a bit far, and you must be exhausted, but if you follow me through this path, it is the quickest route to get us there."

In response, the man did something strange. He reached out and gently began to touch Obinna's face. With both his hands on Obinna's cheeks, he stared very deeply into his eyes for a while, ran his fingers down Obinna's neck and shoulders and held his hands while still staring into his eyes.

Obinna froze with fear, but there was a mysterious warmth in the stranger's palm and a serenity in his eyes which seemed to overcome the fear which he felt.

"What is your name?" the man asked while still holding his hands.

"Obinna," he replied.

"And you are willing to carry my bag to the square for the festival?" he asked as he let go of Obinna's hands.

"Yes, your bag seems heavy and I'm sure you will struggle with it as you've still got a long journey ahead."

The stranger paused for a while, looked fixedly at the bag around Obinna's waist, shook his head and said,

"No, save your energy, you will need lots of it to carry your burden." The stranger pointed in the direction of an iroko tree which had a footpath obscured by small shrubs,

"I will take that route as there are lots of tall trees that cover the sun and its scorching heat on my frail old skin." He waved at Obinna and walked away.

Obinna stood still watching as the man disappeared into the bushes. He was sure that the route the stranger had chosen to go was not the quickest, but he carried on straight ahead as he mumbled to himself,

"Old people, they know what is best, don't they?"

As he walked along, the sounds and the relaxing ambience of the forest made him have flashbacks. That route was familiar to him. He would reach out and touch the hard barks of each tree he recognised. Although he was alone, it felt as if his late father was walking alongside him. They had both walked through those bushes since he was a child, once every year for the festival. Now that he was twenty-five years old, the excitement he felt was still the same.

He recognised the withering palm tree swaying in the wind a few yards away and giggled to himself. It was the tree where Okonga, his father's friend, fell off from many years ago when he tried to impress a lady by offering to tap wine from it on her behalf.

He pointed up at the tree's withered leaves and said:

"I'm sure poor old Okonga will be glad all your leaves have shrivelled." He laughed as he walked over to the tree and caressed its stem as if to say that it was only a joke.

His flashbacks became stronger as there was a peculiar

aroma in the air. It was coconut. He knew he had reached the wooden bridge built over the small river which had its bank lined with coconut trees. The trees would occasionally shed their fruit which falls in the river and, when washed up on dry land, filled the air with the familiar smell which he perceived. But it was not the smell nor the trees which made his heart beat faster; it was the bridge.

That bridge was where his father gave him the oja. He could remember even though he was only one year old at the time. The memory stayed with him, perhaps because the oja became his favourite childhood toy.

His father was a magician who performed petty tricks in the village market square. The villagers loved him but laughed whenever he entertained because they thought that his magic was nothing but deceptions. Obinna's father was persistent in his act and would always tell the villagers that someday, they would stop laughing and believe that he was indeed a magician and that his performance was real and not mere tricks. His father had also told him that he did not have any money nor treasures to give, but the flute was precious. He said to him that if he continued being an honest person, whenever a song is blown into it, believing with all his heart, the flute would conjure magic which would bring amazing things that he could not describe. His father, unfortunately, died twelve years later in his sleep and Obinna was left alone in that mud hut with no parents as his mother passed away while he was being born. He had taught himself how to play that flute, which his father called the oja. It was carved from wood and had a small opening at the top which fits the player's lower lip. It also had three other holes, one at the bottom and two on both sides. He had learned that the hole at the bottom should be left open at all times, and the two holes on the sides are used to control the musical rhythm.

It was with that flute that Obinna earned a living. He would walk daily for miles to the market in Umuzura and entertain people with it and in return, receive silver and copper coins as payment. But he was known never to charge for his entertainment. He believed that his talent was given to him freely by the gods; hence, there was no reason for him to sell what he got for free. Whatever the villagers gave him, he accepted, and if they did not, he would still smile and carry on playing the instrument.

His flashbacks were suddenly interrupted as the bridge swayed in the wind while he was fighting back the tears as he thought of his father. He slowly put his hands in the bag, brought out the flute and began to dance in a coordinated fashion. With his left hand stretched out first, he would take three steps to the left, stretch his right hand and take three steps to the right, raise both in the air and jump up and down like a warrior victorious in battle before blowing into the flute. It felt as if the world stood still, and all his problems had disappeared while he played it. Nothing else mattered.

"Obinna, are you going to cross the bridge, or would you rather stay here and dance all day?" someone shouted behind him as he quickly turned around. It was Igwekala, a middle-aged man, who held the keys that unlocked the hut where they kept the masquerade costumes for the festival. He and Obinna were good friends and shared similar interests in music and dance.

"Sorry Igwekala, I got a bit carried away, and I didn't even know you were on the bridge," Obinna replied with a smile.

"A bit carried away?" Igwekala asked and shook his head, "I have stood here all along, watching you."

"Okay, I was not paying attention then," Obinna replied as he beckoned Igwekala to cross the bridge. "I was thinking about my father," he said as Igwekala got closer. "My heart was heavy, and my eyes were sore from the tears, but when I played my oja, it felt as if these bushes came to comfort me."

Igwekala felt very sorry for Obinna, walked up to him, placed his right hand on his shoulder and said,

"Do not worry, it is all connected; these bushes that came to comfort you is your late father." Igwekala looked up towards the sky and said, "You see, our loved ones die and become the earth underneath our feet, and the earth gives them back to us as this forest that you see, your flute is part of the earth; it is wood, and as you play it, your father lives, hears and dances with you."

Both men smiled and looked at each other while a strong wind swayed the bridge vigorously. Igwekala reached out and touched Obinna's face, and with both hands on his cheeks he looked into his eyes, gently running his palm across Obinna's shoulders before holding his hands and said,

"Now play that song that got you carried away and let us dance with our ancestors, and hurry up, or we will be late to see the beautiful maidens at the festival."

As Obinna played the oja, Igwekala danced hysterically, jokingly pushing him along from the back, as if to get him to hurry up and get to the end of the bridge. Both men suddenly heard a faint grunt from underneath the bridge just as they were about to get to the edge and Igwekala looked down. The sound was from an antelope. It had instantly given birth to a calf. Obinna stopped playing and looked down too.

"This is magical; welcome to Umuzura!" Obinna yelled with joy to the calf as the mother relentlessly licked it from head to toe. He began to play the flute again, but this time, it seemed as if he was trying to entertain the newborn calf. Both men watched as the tired calf's mother tried with much difficulty to stand on its feet. To Obinna, it seemed as though it was enjoying the melody. It stood up and staggered in a series of movements that appeared to mimic Obinna's dance, three steps to the left and three to the right but rather than jumping up and down, the tired antelope tumbled to the ground and looked up at both men.

"Life is beautiful, isn't it?" Obinna said to Igwekala as both men laughed and ran across the bridge as they had realised that they needed to hurry up and get to the festival.

*

Obinna and Igwekala arrived at the village square a bit late. A considerable crowd had started to gather. Men, women and children from Umuzura and some neighbouring villages had begun to pass through the main entrance gates. The gates were handmade from bamboo sticks which stood about twenty feet tall and reinforced with ropes tied to smaller sticks driven into the ground. The smaller sticks served as a fence which they built to encircle the entire arena and they spanned at least 140 feet across. Everyone had to pass through those gates. People at the festival referred to that gate as the 'Gate to Happiness'. Even though the gate was kept wide open and the entrance was free, it was guarded by twelve people, six of whom were powerful women, and the other six were male warriors known as the "*Idanuwo*

Udunre." They were part of a large group of selected and highly trained fearless warriors, entrusted with the duty of protecting the village. But there at Udunre, the warrior's roles were reversed. They gave the women the spears, and the warriors were instead made to carry big baskets of fruits, nuts and wine which they offered to people at the entrance with a smile.

The women and the warriors stood in a line facing each other outside the gates as large crowds of people walked through the middle and went in. Right at the gates were two very young boys, one on each side. They called them the 'Purifiers'. They both held a stick with eagle feathers attached to it and were the last ones to enter the Square. Everyone who approached the boys would kneel before them, lower their heads, and the boys would gently tap the stick six times on the guest's body, three times on the left shoulder and three on the right and usher them in. The two boys at the gates were the ones who decide when those gates should close. They usually allow enough time for guests to enter and as soon as they proceed to tap all twelve people at the gates with their sticks, the gates shut, and anyone else arriving later would not enter the venue.

Obinna and Igwekala passed through the gates. His heart was full of excitement as the loud sounds of the drums and the dust raised by people dancing filled the air. The square had a unique arrangement; small kiosks were built in circles allowing an ample central space. In that space was a large podium. Nobody was allowed to step on it as it was very sacred. It was where the parrot called Udele was allowed to perch and give the villagers 'the prophecy' for the new season. The kiosks served as stalls were food, wine and decorative artwork were sold. It was usually the wealthy merchants that occupied them. Most of the merchants had pot bellies and often wore costly clothes. Everything else in the other stalls was free. People who had cooked the night before would have their food and drinks on display for everyone to enjoy.

The events at Udunre festival followed a specific order. First, it was an older woman called Agbara who was the village's native doctor and sort of the master of the ceremony that speaks, magicians and jesters, perform their tricks, then the maidens dance, the masquerades entertain and finally Udele, the talking parrot delivers the prophecy.

Amidst the chaos, Obinna could see that the purifiers at the gates had summoned for it to shut. He quickly scanned through the large crowd to find Igwekala and inform him that the festival had officially started. He paused and reflected on what was happening for a split second.

"But why would they close a gate called the Gate to Happiness?" he murmured. "Isn't happiness meant for everyone?" he stood still thinking and staring at the gates as they slammed it shut and secured it from inside with a substantial piece of wood that fitted into notches on both sides.

Perhaps happiness is reserved for those who find it, those who are very eager to arrive where it could be found? His thought was interrupted as he could see Igwekala standing in front of one of the kiosks and it seemed he was negotiating with one of the wealthy merchants for the price of a falcon they had on display.

Obinna squeezed through the crowd and ran to Igwekala, dragging him by the arm.

"Come, they have shut the gates and, they are about to start." He noticed that Igwekala was still looking back at the falcon while he dragged him along. "You do remember you have the keys to the kiosk for the masquerade costumes, right?" he asked, to which Igwekala replied,

"Of course, I remember, I have held these keys for many years, so how could I forget?"

Both men stood at a spot where they could see all that was going on. The sounds from the drums intensified as the older woman, Agbara emerged from the crowd.

The entire arena became silent as she pranced around. Little children tried to avoid her by hiding behind their parents as they thought she was very scary. Agbara threw both her hands in the air and started to shake all over as though she was convulsing, dancing to a song which nobody could hear.

Meanwhile, Igwekala was searching through the little bag he had to make sure he still had the keys to the masquerade kiosk.

Agbara summoned the crowd to be quiet with a wave of her right hand, and there was complete silence in the entire arena. She spoke to the crowd with a loud voice.

"Sons and daughters of Umuzura, welcome to Udunre. The dryness has passed, and the rain is here, let those that come with happiness drink to their fill from the fountains of joy, but let those that look upon our ancestors with disdain be forever washed away in its deluge."

The crowd clapped and cheered while the drummers thumped loudly on their instruments. The magicians and jesters ran out from behind the groups; some of them were dwarfs. The dwarfs would occasionally do acrobatic flips, tumble to the ground and square up to each other in what seemed like a wrestling contest. They would throw and purposefully miss punches at their opponents and fall to the ground again and again, and the crowd would roar with laughter each time they did.

Obinna found the magicians fascinating. He particularly liked the tricks they performed with water and fire, so his face lit up as people in the crowd gave them kegs filled with water. They would cover the kegs with palm fronds, mumble a few words which nobody understood and as soon as they lifted the fronds, the water turned to fire.

Some of the magicians were fire-eaters; they would insert dry sticks into the fire and quench the flame by putting it in their mouth.

Obinna's heart began to beat faster as he saw the magicians and jesters make way for the maidens to perform.

Igwekala immediately looked at him with a cheeky smile on his face and said,

"I know you have been waiting for this part all day." It seemed Igwekala was talking to himself as Obinna was distracted.

In Umuzura, some people defined love as the sunrise and sunset, to others it was the wind and its romance with the trees as they sway gently, many say it is the embrace of a child, to Obinna, love was simply Adaure.

Adaure was the lead singer and dancer that performed with the maidens at the festival. Obinna thought her voice was an aphrodisiac. He had become lovestruck from the first time he saw her many years ago by the river that had its banks lined by coconut trees, the same river that had the bridge built over it where his father gave him the oja. She occasionally came there to fetch water. Though their first conversation then was short and cordial, it stayed with him ever since. Obinna had worked out the exact time and days she would come to the river and would always be there waiting for her, and they would talk for what seemed to be hours. He couldn't forget what happened by that river, the day she approached him and told him that she could see great pain and pleasure in his eyes, how she brought out a bottle of olive oil, dipped her finger in it, smeared a little on his forehead and told him that her oil would soothe his pain but as for pleasure, time would tell.

Nobody had ever made him feel that unique, and in Obinna's mind, Adaure was the most crucial part of the Udunre festival.

The crowd was very impressed as she performed. Obinna would wave at her each time she approached where he stood, and she would nod in affirmation but pretend to incorporate the nod in her dance routine.

Igwekala understood what was going on as he and Obinna had discussed earlier the mutual attraction between both of them.

The maidens had performed for about an hour, and it was time for the next act, which was the masquerades. Those masquerades were very mysterious as they believed in Umuzura that it was not humans but rather the spirits of their ancestors who wore the costumes and performed.

The day before the festival, it was Igwekala's duty to go and lock the kiosk where they kept the costumes. Three random witnesses would also be appointed by Agbara to escort Igwekala, and they were there to ensure that, after it was locked, no human eventually sneaked in to wear the costumes overnight and perform the next day.

As the maidens were preparing to leave, Adaure walked towards Obinna and whispered in his ears:

"Meet me now behind the kiosk where the rich merchants are; I would love to speak to you."

Obinna did not hesitate, he clumsily patted himself down and adjusted the small bag tied to his waist, but as soon as he was about to walk away, he heard a voice behind him that firmly said, "You." He turned around and noticed it was Agbara pointing at him and steadily approaching where he stood. The crowd became interested in what was going on and became silent. Adaure carried on walking towards the kiosk where she had asked Obinna to meet him.

Agbara stood in front of Obinna, stretched out her wrinkled hands and touched his face, she placed both her palms on his cheeks and stared deeply into his eyes, as she gently started to run her fingers down his neck and shoulders, Obinna had a very odd sense of déjà vu as she held his hands. He felt that what was happening was oddly similar to his encounter with the thirsty old stranger he met on his way to the festival. The smell from Agbara's clothing, the warmth in her palm and the calmness in her eyes, it all felt very familiar.

"What is your name?" she asked Obinna, "And what have you got in that bag?" she said while pointing at the small bag tied around his waist, Obinna seemed a bit restless as he knew Adaure was waiting for him.

"My name is Obinna, and I've got my oja flute in the bag."

Agbara placed her left arm over his shoulder and with her right hand, she pointed towards the kiosk where the masquerade costumes were kept and replied.

"Behold, our ancestors, they call upon you, they have chosen you to play that your oja while they dance, now it is your duty."

Obinna felt pleased that his ancestors chose him to play for the masquerades, but at that moment, Adaure was more important, he did not want to keep her waiting. He looked at Agbara, shook his head and said:

"Sorry, I have to go where my heart beats; please let the ancestors choose someone else," and he started to walk away.

"Umuzura is what sustains your heartbeat," Agbara responded as she looked at Obinna in disappointment. "Is there anyone else who is willing? Our ancestors will not be kept waiting."

Somebody in the crowd raised his hand and offered to play for the masquerades but with a bamboo flute, and Agbara summoned Igwekala to unlock the kiosk and let the masquerades out.

Igwekala unlocked the kiosk, and the masquerades jumped out. Some people in the crowd moved further away while others clapped and cheered them along. The masquerades usually danced uniquely, they would roll in the sand and their costumes would be seen as a mere pile of dry clothing, as though what wore them had disappeared, and then they would come to life and stand tall again.

Obinna squeezed through some spectators and saw Adaure waiting behind the kiosk where they intended to meet. She sat on the floor, taking off her neck beads and armbands as he approached. Even though she heard him coming, she did not make eye contact immediately so as not to make it apparent that she was eagerly waiting.

Obinna sat down by her side, and they did not speak for

a short while. She broke the silence as she looked at him from the corner of her eyes, smiled and said:

"Agbara, she requested you to do something, right?"

"Yes, she said our ancestors chose me to play the oja while the masquerades performed," he replied.

"And why did you not accept the offer?" she asked. "It is a great honour to be chosen by our ancestors."

"Yes, I understand Adaure, but it is a greater honour to be chosen by you, and the song I bring with me says that all is complete when you are here."

Adaure hugged him and placed her forehead against his as that was a unique way people show affection in Umuzura. Both of them felt totally at peace, like two drunkards inebriated by their favourite wine; they were completely unaware of their surroundings.

*

The sun had already set, and tall, gloomy shadows could be seen cast in the sand by the dusk as the masquerades finished their performance.

Igwekala picked up the costumes from the ground, folded them neatly in a pile and proceeded to lock them in the kiosk.

"Udele, the parrot, will deliver the prophecy soon," Adaure whispered into Obinna's ears as it seemed he was about to fall asleep on her shoulders.

"I'm a bit worried about what the prophecy will be," she said while holding her jaw with both hands. "We have had the message about the terrible floods which destroyed many of our crops a couple of years ago, and I hope this year will be better."

"The prophecies have not all been doom and gloom," Obinna replied, "remember when Udele told us about the big cassava harvest; how our lands became fertile and our farmers enjoyed a whole year of surplus harvest and sales? It will always be well with us Adaure, we all lived through it," he said with a smile. "Come, let us move closer so we can see and hear it all."

Agbara emerged from the crowd accompanied by the two young boys. One of the boys carried a cage covered with black clothing and in that cage was the parrot, Udele. The other boy had a scroll, a small brush and ink which he would use to write the prophecy as it was delivered.

There was complete silence in the crowd as everyone knew that the prophecy was the last and most crucial part of the festival.

As the three approached the podium built in the centre of the arena, the parrot began to say "Prophecy, prophecy," continuously. It did not seem to be able to say anything else.

The villagers were not surprised as they knew the parrot would speak after Agbara completed her ritual.

The boy with the cage stepped on the podium and placed it on a stand built specifically for it, Agbara held the other boy's hand, and they both walked around the podium three times, she looked at the crowd, requested everyone to kneel and instructed the boy on the podium to remove the cloth covering the cage and release the bird.

Udele, the parrot, was released; it was a female grey parrot with large white patches in the feathers around its eyes. The bird flapped and spread its wings, perched on the highest part of the podium and began to speak, and this was the prophecy it delivered:

Over many rivers have I flown
To dance with this whirlwind that has blown
But I would not have, had I known
That this whirlwind has an evil plan of its own
Yes, it will explode with such hate
It will kill you all; it will be your doomed fate
Make friends now with the ashes and the dust
because only them can you trust
For after the grief, ashes and dust you will all become when you die
The price you must all pay because the truth which you knew will soon become a lie.

*

It had become dark outside as the dusk made way for the night. The sky had become decorated with myriads of stars, and the sound of crickets chirping masked the eerie silence. The parrot had delivered the prophecy and the festival that year had come to an end.

They opened the gates, and guests started to leave. Everyone looked worried and confused as they went home. People in small groups discussed and tried to make sense of the prophecy; they knew the message was a bad omen but were not exactly sure how or when it would affect their lives.

Obinna, Adaure and Igwekala were amongst the last ones to leave, the journey home felt longer, and Obinna noticed Igwekala was staring at the ground as they walked home.

"Are you okay?" Obinna asked him. "You have been silent for too long." Igwekala sighed as he struggled to respond; it seemed he was more troubled than Obinna and Adaure.

"That bird said we are all going to die," Igwekala replied. "I do not want to die; we must find a way to avert this calamity whatever it might be."

Obinna rubbed Igwekala's shoulder to comfort him while Adaure walked alongside both men.

"Igwekala, all that is born will surely die, to die now or to die later are the same," Obinna responded. "The fear of death is the first step taken towards that journey to the grave."

"But it is human to fear," Igwekala objected. "I do not feel good about all this, I sense danger, what are we going to do?"

Obinna shook his head with pity and wrapped his arms around Igwekala and Adaure's shoulders to reassure them.

"I do not know what we should do about the prophecy," he responded, "but what I know for now is that we are alive, so now that we are breathing, I have an idea of what we could do."

"So, what should we do?" Igwekala and Adaure asked simultaneously as they both stopped abruptly, eagerly interested in his response.

"We should dance," Obinna replied with a big smile on his face.

"Dance?" Igwekala queried and looked very confused. "Did he just say dance?" he asked, looking at Adaure who was trying very hard not to laugh, "Seriously, Obinna are you crazy?" he carried on as Adaure burst into laughter.

"Yes, he said we should dance, you heard him correctly," she clarified.

Adaure's laughter and the big grin on Obinna's face seemed to frustrate him even more. The surprised look on Igwekala's face became even more apparent as he stood with his mouth wide open, staring at both in disbelief.

"Udele's prophecy is that we are going to perish somehow, and your great solution is that we dance?" Igwekala carried on.

"Yes Igwekala, I said dance," Obinna replied while still smiling, "Come on, look at the skies," he said as he pointed upwards. "Do you see those stars?" he asked. "They are our audience, and this is our stage," he continued as he became very dramatic, dancing and spreading both his arms apart, took three steps to the right, away from Adaure and Igwekala, and three to the left towards them, reached into the small bag he had all along and brought the oja out. He would play the flute and pause as he spoke.

"Go on Igwekala, dance for our audience," Obinna continued as Adaure had already started dancing.

Igwekala was not interested at all initially but gradually started to give in to Obinna's demand. He remembered how he had convinced him to dance and play the oja amidst his sadness on that bridge they crossed to get to the festival. The melody from the oja was perfect as Obinna played it and Igwekala slowly started nodding.

"You can do better than that," Obinna coaxed, and Igwekala became fully involved. He and Adaure danced their hearts out as they encircled Obinna who carried on playing. A few people who were on their way home from the festival stopped to see what the excitement was all about, but they couldn't make sense of it all.

"It must be all that free palm wine they drank at Udunre," some suggested. "Hope they get home safely."

*

Obinna bade farewell to Igwekala as they crossed the bridge on their way home. That night, Adaure and Obinna went back to his hut. They were so carried away with their conversation, and she was not very keen to go back home.

As soon as they got in, she went straight to his wooden bed and relaxed. The journey home and all that dancing at the festival had worn her out. He knew it was best to end the conversation at that point so that she could rest.

Obinna slowly walked to the window and propped it open with a bamboo stick, looked outside into the darkness and noticed that it had started to drizzle. He scooped some nuts left in his metal pan, threw a few in his mouth and was eagerly waiting for the birds to sing so he could feed them, but that night, the birds were silent. He sat there thinking about all that had happened that day. He thought about the strange older man he met on his way and wondered if he ever made it to the festival at all. He was not sure if the stray dogs that greeted him that morning were part of an omen. He remembered his encounter with Igwekala on the bridge and the antelope that gave birth as he played the oja. He failed to find any connection between those events. A part of him felt responsible for the curse from Udele. Perhaps if he had agreed to play the oja for the masquerades, maybe the prophecy would have been different, he thought.

"You need to come and rest," Adaure whispered, and he

got up, walked over to her and lay by her side.

As they both lay, he could feel there was something strange about that night. The rain had stopped abruptly; the birds outside had nothing to say, but the silence was disturbed by the energy radiating from two lovebirds who had a lot to tell each other.

Chapter Two

One month had passed, and news about the prophecy had spread across the three neighbouring villages to Umuzura. In the east was Umunede, most of its indigenes were skilled blacksmiths.

To the west was *Kanuri*, a village of animal farmers whose ruler was known as King Nuri, and in the north was *Tangandoom*, a village of warlords whose king was known as Gandoom.

Umuzura was in the south and had the smallest landmass and inhabitants compared to its neighbours. They did not have a king but instead had a group of elders who made the crucial decisions in the village.

Over the previous years, they had sustained a cordial relationship between the villages in the south, east and west but did not know much about Tangandoom, in the north.

The northerners lived an isolated life and were not known to be men and women of honour. The nearby villages had made several attempts to reach out to Gandoom, their king, without any success. Messengers and gift bearers had been sent in the past to try and convince him to cooperate with his neighbours, but all efforts failed as he seized the messengers sent to him and held them as prisoners.

Gandoom believed he was a god and everyone in Tangandoom were direct descendants of his noble bloodline.

Those who were not of that bloodline, he believed, have been born to be his subjects hence he sought to understand and master the art of warfare, magic and traditional medicine to fortify his territory and expand his influence.

Gandoom's knowledge of magic and medicine had enabled him to train an army of giants, mighty warriors and an executioner who they feared across the region. Even though others did not know a lot about Tangandoom, their king knew everything he needed to know about the other villages as he had spies who he sent out to acquire as much information as they could. To the neighbouring communities, Gandoom and his people were nothing more than a problem and mystery that is best left alone and unsolved.

*

It was the seventh day of the week which the villagers commemorated as the busiest market day in Umuzura. The sun had risen, and slow-moving clouds were apparent in the skies, decorated with rays of bright colours. The elders had scheduled their weekly meeting in the village hall where they discussed the affairs of the village but most importantly, the prophecy.

During the meeting which commenced a few hours before midday, twelve elders and three messengers sat and pondered over the interpretation of the parrot's message but could not entirely understand it. They focused on discussing the whirlwind that would bring pain and suffering to the village and what it might be. Some said it would be a disease while others suggested it was famine or war. As they reviewed the decisions that have been made to ensure that they prepared the village for whatever might happen, one of the elders stood up and proposed:

"My fellow elders, we have done all that is within our might, we have requested that all farmers in the village contribute a quarter of their harvest to the community for storage so, in the event of famine, we will have enough to feed everyone till it is over."

All the elders nodded in affirmation as they looked at each other and agreed that it was the right thing to do.

Another elder stood up, cleared his throat by coughing and added:

"We have instructed our warriors to watch over the village day and night to protect us, but I suggest we need more men and women to be trained just in case we are besieged by war, we do not have enough warriors."

Some of the elders nodded and agreed while others were sceptical and shook their heads. There were divided opinions in the room, as several elders started to debate openly regarding the suggestion.

The noise was interrupted as one elder stood and objected:

"No, Umuzura does not believe in war, it is not our way of life, and I suggest that the Idanuwo warriors we already have are enough, for now, let us ensure that our herbalists and healers are encouraged to seek after the best medicines in case we have a disease outbreak."

The discussion was interrupted by a high-pitched voice that suddenly interjected:

"Listen, everyone, my problem is that parrot." The rest of the elders looked to see who was speaking as they did not expect that suggestion.

The elder speaking was a man whose name was Ekwueme. He was known to be temperamental and outspoken. His clothes never seemed to fit as he was very short and would hold the part of his garment that wrapped around his waist with one hand so it would not fall off. Ekwueme was always drunk and would defend his habits by claiming that they never ridicule people who eat a lot in the village; hence, they should extend the same gesture to those who drink excessively.

People in the village called him 'the drunkard' but never to his face.

The elders tried very hard to conceal their laughter as some hid their faces with their palms. It was apparent to them that he was a bit drunk that morning.

The drunkard carried on and staggered to the centre of the gathering to get more attention.

"Yes, that parrot called Udele is my problem, and she is the reason for all this trouble."

"So, what are you suggesting we do about Udele then?" an elder asked, to which he replied with a slur:

"Yes listen, we need to convince her to shut up, I have had enough of these prophecies." He tried to walk back to his seat but could not figure out where it was as he almost sat on someone else's legs. An elder stood up, held his arm and helped him back to where he sat previously.

The man who helped him added:

"Udele's prophecy is part of our tradition, our forefathers listened to her, and even when this particular bird dies as you all know, another parrot will be chosen by Agbara to carry on the tradition."

The meeting lasted for about an hour after which they

cast a vote on the issues discussed, and adhered to the decisions in which most people support. The three messengers present were also instructed to go and spread the word about their conclusions to the villagers and seek their opinion on the problems they discussed. All those present at the meeting got up, greeted one another and left the room hurriedly so those who wanted to attend the village market could get there on time.

*

It was midday when Obinna had finished preparations and was ready to leave his hut for the market day. He preferred to arrive a bit late to ensure he would have more spectators when he performs with the flute.

"I'm sure today will go well," he said as he gave the oja one last wipe with a piece of cloth and checked all its holes for blockages. "I hope people at the market will be generous too because I'm running out of money; hopefully, I should earn enough today to last me for the next couple of months."

He walked towards the window, took one last look outside to see if the skies were clear and placed the oja and some water in his small bag which he tied around his waist and left his hut.

He felt very excited as he whistled to himself and walked along. The excitement he felt was because he knew that Adaure would be there at the market, and that made his journey seem shorter. He was surprised when he started to perceive that familiar aroma of coconut in the air as he did not expect to get to the bridge that soon and as he looked ahead, he could see the bridge being swayed by a gentle breeze which felt rather chilly for a bright sunny day.

He decided to distract himself from the flashbacks he usually got on that bridge by playing a song with the oja.

It was an excellent way to practice before he got to the market, he thought.

He reached into his bag for the flute and stepped on the bridge, stood still for a while to look at the beautiful view of the river and the distant landscape.

The moment he tried to blow into it, he heard a loud noise above and looked up to see a large group of crows cowing as they flew overhead past him. It seemed to him that the birds were distressed. He wondered where they came from, knowing fully well that crows were rare in the village, let alone a group that large. While he watched the birds as they flew, he moved closer to the edge of the bridge to hold on to its wooden rails, a strong gust of wind had started to shake the bridge vigorously. From where he stood, he noticed the birds were flying towards the north and had conglomerated in the air, flying in concentric circles around a whirlwind. The wind spun debris of leaves and dust as it blew, and it seemed the crows were at war with the wind as they were flapping their wings hysterically, attacking the debris it carried.

A sudden chill ran down his spine while he watched what was going on, his palms became sweaty, and he could barely stand erect. He knew that what he was seeing was unusual. Obinna felt sick to his stomach and could feel a cold sweat trickling down the side of his forehead; his sweaty palms made it very difficult to hold the oja which slipped from his grasp and fell on the wooden bridge.

As he struggled to bend over and pick it up, his entire

body felt numb, and he fell flat on his face and passed out. In that state of unconsciousness, he could still hear and see with the mind's eye. It seemed as if he saw Udele the parrot perched on the edge of the bridge with her wings spread out. The parrot's beak was not moving, but he could hear her voice talking to him, repeating phrases from the prophecy, and she kept saying,

"This whirlwind has an evil plan of its own; it will kill you all; it will be your doomed fate."

The parrot's voice and the sounds from the crows echoing in his head started to fade away as he slowly regained consciousness. He realised when he opened his eyes that the whirlwind had stopped and the crows were no longer there, but the feeling of nausea and shock he experienced continued to prevail.

He tried as hard as he could to get back on his feet, gasping for air with a dazed look, and could not understand what had just happened to him, but knew that he needed to inform as many people as possible about what he had seen. He used the edge of the bridge to support himself as he picked the oja up and stood.

I must get to the market quickly and inform everyone, this which I have just seen is undoubtedly a bad sign, he thought and ran as fast he could.

The intensity of what he felt made him unable to realise that his sandals had cut loose, and he was running barefoot, thistles had torn the soles of his feet, and the blood that oozed from the wound went completely unnoticed. He did not care about routes and directions as he darted through the thick forest, unaware of the paths that would get him there quicker.

He was out of breath when he got to the mahogany trees

that separated him from the market square, so he hid behind one of the trees to observe what was going on. From where he was, he could hear the earth-shaking as if a thousand horses had been let loose in the square. He tried to walk a bit closer so he could see beyond the dense leaves that obstructed his view but could not as the pain from the wounds in his feet became more intense, so he decided to crawl along.

The square was in full view as he crawled and peeked through the leaves and what he saw was indeed horses, black stallions whose eyes were red like burning furnaces. He could see that some of the horses were attached to wooden chariots, very tall fierce-looking warriors rode the horses, they had a tattoo of the rising sun drawn on their chests and each held a spear. He noticed that the rest of them were on foot and held shields in one hand and swords in the other. Their shields also had a symbol of the rising sun engraved in it. Obinna knew that those warriors were from Tangandoom, the village in the north as he had heard stories about the giants from the north who had the rising sun engraved in their chests and were indestructible.

He could hear the agonising screams of women and children calling out for help while the warriors ordered them to sit down on the floor, raise their hands and surrender to their demands.

He knew that for those men to have made it that far, it meant that the warriors that guard the entrance to Umuzura would have fallen. His village, Umuzura had been conquered, and he was right there in the middle of it all, helplessly watching as it unfolded.

Obinna thought the best thing to do was to hide and stay

out of sight, or perhaps it would be better for him to run away in the opposite direction or fight with all the energy left in him. He felt it was wrong to hide there and watch his people being slain or perhaps taken as prisoners for whatever reason those warriors had besieged them.

He looked at himself from the shoulders down to his feet to see if he had anything that looked slightly like a weapon to defend himself with as he was strongly considering fighting, but all he could see was the oja still in that bag tied firmly around his waist.

The men from Tangandoom had almost taken full control of the square; the villagers from Umuzura had all been rounded up, tied and were told to stand in a straight line.

Obinna could see that the warriors had separated into two groups, one group ensured the prisoners obeyed while the rest who were on horses rode into the village. The ones headed to the village also separated into two groups and rode towards the east and west respectively. It seemed they knew the geography of the village and were trying to avoid the river and the bridge by riding around it.

Obinna heard a voice screaming for help and saw that it was a woman being dragged around by the warriors. He immediately recognised the sound, and when he looked, he noticed that it was Adaure. She had managed to break away from the line in an attempt to flee but had been subdued and dragged back to join the rest of the prisoners. Looking at Adaure screaming for help broke Obinna's heart, he could no longer hide while they pushed her around, he reached into the bag tied around his waist, grabbed the oja and jumped out from where he was hiding. That flute carved from wood felt like a sword in Obinna's hands, it was his word against theirs, so he charged towards the warrior holding Adaure, knowing fully well that though he did not stand a chance, at least he gave it his best.

"Please leave her alone!" he screamed at the warrior while waving the oja frantically. "Leave her alone, I beg of you," he demanded, and they all looked at him in disbelief.

One of them ordered the warrior who Obinna confronted not to use his sword as he wanted to be sure that what Obinna had in his hands was indeed a flute.

He walked towards Obinna who was now breathing very heavily, looked at him from head to toe, reached out, grabbed him by the wrist and raised his arm to have a closer look at the oja to make sure it was not a weapon.

There was an awkward, prolonged silence when the warrior looked at the flute. It was as if the warrior had been hypnotised by it.

Obinna held on to the oja and refused to let go. He was confident that he saw fury quickly turn to fear in that warrior's eyes as he looked at the oja.

"Look at what we have here," the warrior said to the others, "he believes he can defeat Gandoom's warriors with a flute, look," he said, pointing at it.

Obinna remained calm. It was apparent to him that the warrior was highly ranked amongst the group as he could see that while he spoke, the rest paid very keen attention and were willing to act upon his commands.

"All right, come on then great soldier, I want you to defeat me," the warrior continued, "fight me with your dangerous flute," he joked.

After he beckoned him to fight, three of his comrades surrounded Obinna, one pushed him towards the warrior and said:

"You do what the executioner says, did you not hear him?"

Obinna shook his head.

"I don't want to fight you," he said, and put the oja back in his bag.

The warrior who challenged Obinna to the duel became very upset, struck him in the jaw with clenched fists, and he tumbled to the ground. He watched as he got up and hit him again, but this time, harder than before.

As he fell, Adaure pleaded with him to stay down.

"Please, do not get up," she said, "do not put yourself at risk, they will kill you."

The villagers began to sigh to show disapproval for what they were doing to him.

Obinna got up again and refused to stay down. The warrior became very frustrated with what was happening and responded:

"All right, I'm going to ask you one last time to challenge me to a duel because if you refuse, I am going to kill her now, while you watch." He pointed at Adaure.

Obinna knew he meant every word he said. He stood tall, breathing heavily and was very nervous.

He looked at Adaure, who was shaking her head in disapproval and accepted the challenge.

"Okay I will fight you, please spare her, I will fight."

Obinna clutched onto the bag where he placed the oja and began to beg his dead ancestors for help in his mind. He thought that something terrible would happen, but he would rather it occurred to him than his beloved Adaure, who was already in tears and struggling to break away from the warriors who held her back.

The warrior looked at him with disdain and smiled as he walked majestically in circles around Obinna and said:

"Men, when will you ever learn?" he continued as he faced the villagers and his comrades like an orator delivering a speech. "You see, this is your problem, always willing to die for love."

He had figured out that Adaure and Obinna were perhaps emotionally attached.

"A little while ago, you were willing to fight and protect her, risking your own life, but after I invited you to the challenge, you declined." He bellowed and paused as if he wanted what he had said to sink into everyone's head and continued:

"But as soon as I threatened to slay her, all of a sudden, you accepted the challenge." He stopped speaking again and looked around.

"I do not understand men and why you do the things you do when love or lust is involved," he carried on.

"I was not willing to fight only for love," Obinna interrupted, "I was willing to fight for a human, we love because we are human."

He made eye contact with Adaure as he spoke as if to reassure her that it will be okay and looked at his villagers whose hands were all tied behind their backs.

"I would do the same for anyone of my people held here as prisoners," he promised.

"Yes, we are human," the warrior interrupted, "but love? what nonsense, the world we humans live in is like a forest, and in that forest, either you eat, or something will eat you," he argued. "Me, I chose to eat," he concluded, thumped his chest twice as he charged towards Obinna and said, "Now defend yourself because I am going to devour you."

Amidst the fear, Obinna pulled the oja out of his bag, not entirely sure whether to try and use it like a knife or throw it at the warrior and flee.

He staggered and became even more afraid as the warrior cracked his knuckles and neck and approached.

Obinna was now speaking to his ancestors loudly while holding the oja. He staggered again, took three steps to the left and three to the right, looked towards the sky and said, "Great ancestors, I want to live, we all do, please help me."

And he felt an unusual energy surge through him, the oja he held felt like it had just been put through fire as it felt hot, thick grey clouds gathered overhead, and lightning struck as the earth shook with it.

Adaure's eyes lit up with hope as she nodded and screamed with joy,

"Obinna they heard you, our ancestors heard you, they are here with us!"

The earth shook even more as the warrior who charged Obinna became distracted. He looked and could see his comrades who rode into Obinna's village, riding back on their horses.

Obinna's heartbeat was in unison with the sounds the horse's hooves made as they rode back.

"We succeeded, we left a few of our men behind to bring the rest of the prisoners," one of them said to the warrior who was ready to fight.

The warrior ignored Obinna for a while and spoke to his comrade.

"Good, our king, Gandoom, will honour you all when

we get back to Tangandoom."

He took one last look at Obinna and walked away towards one of the men on horses, who had already dismounted and had a cage covered with black clothing. The warrior took it from the man that held it, removed the cloth and smiled when he saw what was inside. It was Udele, the parrot that delivered the prophecy. He opened the cage, picked the bird up by its legs to observe it and raised his arms high as he marvelled at its beauty.

The parrot raised its head high, flapped and spread its wings, looked straight at Obinna as it squawked and said "Prophecy, prophecy," while lightning and thunder struck simultaneously.

When they stared at each other, Obinna felt that Udele was responsible for all the calamity that had befallen his village that day. It was undoubtedly Udele's fulfilled prophecy that got Umuzura in the mess they were all in. Then he had fully understood that the whirlwind which Udele said would blow from the north and kill them all was Gandoom's warriors.

"So, this must be the bird we have heard that dictates how these villagers live their lives," the warrior queried while observing Udele.

"Yes, it must be, as it was the only bird we found in the village," his comrade responded. "They say this bird is significant, and it has magical powers and even speaks like a human," he added.

"Speaks like a human?" the warrior asked while shaking his arm on which Udele perched as if to encourage the bird to talk. "It cannot talk, it only repeats certain words they say to it," he said, as he tried opening the bird's beak to look down its throat. "A useless bird that dictates to an entire village what they should and shouldn't do?" he muttered. "No wonder this village is so weak and unproductive, this bird talks to them in their heads and they stupidly believe they can hear it speaking."

"I think the only thing this bird will be good for is bird pepper soup cooked with goat kidneys," he joked. "But I am sure the king loves animals and would prefer to keep it," he suggested, as he handed Udele back to his comrade and demanded they put the parrot back in the cage.

The warrior had been distracted and had almost forgotten about Obinna, who stood there watching silently.

"All right, get them all organised in a straight line while we wait for the rest of the prisoners," he instructed, "and you, I will spare your life today because I am under orders from our king to bring as many of you alive as possible," he admitted to Obinna and walked away towards the rest of his men.

"Tangandoom needs workers," he continued with his hands crossed at the back, walking around the prisoners slowly but majestically, "So you all are now workers and will work for Gandoom, who is now your king."

The warriors who rode into the village returned with the rest of the prisoners they could find.

They instructed Obinna to join the line of prisoners, and his hands were tied up. But he had ensured his oja was safely placed in the bag around his waist before he was tied. He scanned through the entire group to see who was there or had been left behind and there amongst them was Igwekala, the man who held the keys to the masquerade costumes at Umuzura's festival. It appeared he was limping due to an injury on his right leg.

He saw Agbara, the older woman who was their native doctor, holding the young boys known as the purifiers, each in one hand. When he looked at her face, he knew she was extremely exhausted, but he could see hope in her eyes as she and the young boys were smiling and humming a song nobody could understand as the warriors led them on.

He saw their warriors, the Idanuwo Udunre who guarded the gates at their festival, but noticed there were only six women amongst them. Obinna wondered what happened to the other six men.

"Perhaps they had all been killed?" he murmured.

He could see the maidens who danced with Adaure as they were terrified and appeared to clutch the arms of some men as they walked along. The men they held unto were the wealthy merchants at the festival. Those merchants were the most distressed. From the look in their faces, it seemed their world had come to an end. To them, hope was implausible. They lived for the moment.

Amongst the group, they tied only the men's hands. The women and children were allowed to walk freely but under close supervision by the warriors.

Obinna heard a high-pitched voice somewhere in the group and saw a man who fell on the floor, wriggling and looking up at the skies. The man was Ekwueme, the elder who was always drunk, as he continued with his usual effronteries.

"It is Udele, that evil parrot has brought this upon us all!" he cried, "I warned you all, but you would not listen," he maintained, "I warned you all to get rid of that parrot."

Udele, the parrot covered in the cage began to say

repetitively, "Prophecy, prophecy," as Ekwueme looked at it, shook his head and cried even louder as they forced him to stand up and continue walking.

The warrior who led the group appeared with his hands still crossed at the back.

"Enough of this nonsense now," he interrupted. "The sun has set, and it looks like the winds will bring rain upon us, we must move," he warned. "The journey is still far."

Chapter Three

And that journey was indeed very far. Six hundred miles of fertile and barren land, from the tropical rain forest, where the tall trees bowed in the harsh winds as if they said, "*This journey will shake you but be resilient*," to the savanna region where the dry grasslands, shrubs and short trees full of thorns stretched out to meet the desert, which hummed tunes of prolonged suffering to their ears at night.

They did suffer during that journey. The warriors gave them food during the day, but the food was very rationed as the warriors who led them got the lion's share. Water was scarce. They drank only three cups per day and Obinna, on several occasions had to go days without water as he would give his to the elderly ones or the children.

On certain days he would carry Igwekala on his back as the wound he sustained on his leg from one of the warrior's spears had become infected and made it almost impossible for him to walk.

The warrior who led the group gave Obinna a new pair of sandals to protect his feet but had warned him never to speak to Adaure during the journey; he told him that if he disobeyed, the consequence would be death, so all he could do was to talk to her with his eyes.

And Adaure understood it all. She and Obinna communicated with unspoken words. When he blinked during the day, it meant "Carry on my love," and when his eyes closed at night, it said "Goodnight."

Each nod had its meaning, each cough drew her attention, and each sigh conveyed a message. A message of love, perseverance and hope.

*

The journey took thirty days. They walked during the day and slept at night. It took them longer as they were slowed down by the injured and the elderly. A few of his villagers could not carry on, and they left their dead bodies as food for the vultures. Those who continued were dehydrated and weak, and some wished they died while they slept.

Igwekala's leg had become worse, and Obinna had to carry him for the rest of the journey. He refused to let his friend die in the middle of nowhere.

The warriors did not stop him from carrying Igwekala. The one who led the group untied their hands to make it easier for him to help Igwekala but would occasionally look at Obinna and wonder how much longer he was willing to lift his friend.

Obinna could hardly breathe as they passed some rocky terrain. From the landscape, he sensed that their destination, Tangandoom was not too far away. They had walked for twenty-eight days, but he was not entirely sure how much longer the journey would take.

The warriors had untied all the men and ordered everyone to rest before they proceeded.

"Obinna, please leave me here," Igwekala pleaded, "You will not make it if you don't leave me."

Obinna's vision had become blurry from fatigue. He knew what Igwekala said was true. There was no way he would make it while carrying him on his back, but he did not have a choice, he believed in honour and knew right from wrong, he would not leave his friend to die there.

"No Igwekala," Obinna replied, "I am not going to leave you," he objected. "Today you are my burden, I will carry you and if we live through it, perhaps tomorrow you will carry someone else's."

"No Obinna, there is no tomorrow," Igwekala sobbed, "Look up there," he said, pointing towards the skies at a group of vultures circling above, "those birds are following us, they are waiting for me to die so they can feast on my flesh."

Obinna looked up at the birds and gently placed Igwekala on the ground. The fact that Igwekala had given up hope broke his heart.

"Yes, Igwekala, I can see them," he replied. "Those birds are not here to feast on your flesh," he reassured. "They are our audience, and this is our stage," he asserted and gently placed his hands on Igwekala's shoulders.

Obinna became dramatic like a performer observed by a large crowd, took two steps away from Igwekala, three to the left and three to the right and pulled out the oja from the bag tied around his waist.

He would play a short song with the oja and pause abruptly to encourage Igwekala.

"Igwekala, they are watching us; they are learning," Obinna continued as he spread both his arms apart, dancing with coordinated movements.

"Stand up, let us teach them the rhythm of our ancestors,

that harmony that brings clouds together and serenades Umuzura with gentle rain."

The warrior leading the group watched what was happening all along. He was keen and curious to understand the dialogue between both of them.

Igwekala had already started smiling as Obinna entertained him. He forced himself to stand on his feet and joined the dance even though he was limping.

Both men were all smiles as they danced. Igwekala looked up at the vultures again while Obinna played the oja, and he could see the birds flying in perfect circles, organised and flapping their wings in sync with the notes Obinna was playing.

Both men hugged each other and nodded. Igwekala became full of energy which he could not understand where it had come from and started walking and limping alongside Obinna unassisted.

"Enough now!" the warrior who led the group bellowed. "You two must sit down now; we have two more days to walk before we get to Tangandoom."

"So, you are a flautist?" he asked. "Show me that flute again," he demanded as he walked towards Obinna and Igwekala.

Obinna handed the oja to him as instructed. He hoped that the warrior did not intend to destroy it or keep it for himself.

"What type of flute is this?" the warrior asked.

"It is an oja," Obinna replied. "My father gave it to me when I was a child." He tried to show the warrior how to hold it and how the holes are covered to produce musical notes, but the warrior objected.

"Keep your hands to yourself," he instructed as he continued observing. "So your father gave you this, eh?" he asked.

"Yes," Obinna replied.

"And where is your father now?" he queried and looked at Obinna with keen interest.

"He died when I was a boy; my mother is also dead; she died while I was being born," he replied.

The warrior did not say a word for a while and crossed his hands at the back, still holding on to the oja as he walked away. He turned around and looked at Obinna and signalled him to come with a wave of his right hand.

"Come here; I will show you something," he said and walked towards his horse as Obinna followed. He reached into a saddle that hung on his horse's back and drew a sword.

Obinna stood still; he was not sure what the warrior's intentions were.

The warrior gently pulled the sword out of its leather sheath, exposing its shiny blades and spoke while observing it very carefully. He led Obinna away from his horse as he talked to him.

"My father gave me this sword too before he died in battle."

He swung the sword left and right as if to show Obinna how to use it.

"His gift to me is precious," he continued. "You see, with this sword, I ward off enemies and became Gandoom's executioner." He looked at Obinna and very calmly placed the sword back in its scabbard, walked back to his horse and put the sword back in the saddle where he got it from, walked a few steps towards Obinna and said,

"Your father's gift to you has less value than mine because wherever you go, a sword will always defeat a flute," he concluded, threw the oja back to him and ordered his men to lead the prisoners.

*

Obinna and his villagers were not allowed to sleep that night. The warrior who led them had given the order to continue their journey through the night as Tangandoom was not very far off. The warrior had figured out from observing the clouds that gathered above that heavy rain was expected, and if they carried on through the night, they would get to their destination before the thunderstorms.

It was the early hours in the morning when they approached a vast expanse of cornfields. The fields covered about ten acres of land and had paths that ran through it. Obinna could not see very clearly as the early morning fog was thick, but he could feel the wetness of the dew that had settled on the leaves caress his skin as they stumbled through. It made him feel a bit better. He was exhausted as Igwekala had become almost like a dead weight on his back. He was not moving at all and had passed out earlier on, but Obinna continued to talk to him to encourage him to hang on. Obinna knew Igwekala was still alive because he could feel his heartbeat on his shoulder and occasionally, he would drift in and out of consciousness, murmur a few words and pass out again.

"Igwekala, you will make it," he continued to reassure his friend, "stay strong, you will make it."

Obinna had concluded in his mind that those cornfields

were human-made as he observed the way they grew the crops in perfectly straight lines. He was sure the paths that ran through them had been created to allow access to farmers or whoever worked in the fields. But he wondered who owned the fields and why it was located in the middle of nowhere and near Tangandoom.

His curiosity was satisfied when the warrior who led them reached into the saddle that hung around his horse's back, pulled out an ivory horn and spoke to his comrade.

"I will announce our presence now, so our men from Tangandoom will know we have arrived at our cornfields."

Obinna had understood from what the warrior said that the king, Gandoom, owned the fields, and he was sure that they had almost gotten to their destination.

The warrior blew into the horn three times with his head tilted backwards, placed it back in the saddle and ordered his men to wait.

Obinna gently placed Igwekala on the ground and waited with the rest of his villagers as they could hear a loud horn sounding in the distance in response to the horn signal given by the warrior who led them.

"Where are we?" Igwekala asked him as he suddenly regained consciousness but looked dazed and confused.

Obinna did not have enough time to answer the question as they could hear the sounds of some horse's hooves as it got louder. Both men looked and saw five horsemen riding towards them, each was bare-chested, and he could see the tattoo of the rising sun on their chests.

The horsemen dismounted and ran to the warrior who was leading the group with great excitement. They bowed and hugged him with a smile.

"Executioner, welcome home," one of the men remarked, "we have been looking forward to your return."

"Executioner, are these the prisoners from Umuzura and did we lose any of our men?" the other one asked as he looked at Obinna's villagers.

"It is more appropriate that we refer to them as workers for now," the warrior who was with Obinna replied. "They have all obeyed my commands so far, the moment they disobey then they will become prisoners," he countered, "No, Umuzura is weak, and we trounced them with no casualties."

The men got back on their horses and nodded at the warrior who Obinna understood that perhaps he was known as the executioner.

The men rode towards Tangandoom and Obinna, and the rest followed. They had reached the last row of the cornfields when he suddenly experienced an odd sense of déjà vu. He could hear laughter and conversations in the distance, and looking further ahead, he saw a big gate carved from gold. The gate's reinforcements and fences were also made of gold, and it stretched out in both directions. He could hear drummers as well as musical instruments and could see two young boys standing at those gates holding long whips. Six very tall men also stood next to the boys, and each had a long spear in one arm.

Obinna started having flashbacks as they approached the gates. It felt as if he was passing through the gates, back home at the Udunre festival.

The sounds from the drums, the warriors at the gates and the young boys all made him feel as if he was home.

As they passed through, the boys would whip each person that walked past them and say:

"This is your pain, and this is our sympathy."

Obinna did not feel the pain when he passed through the gates. Their whips on his body went unnoticed. There was a fire in his eyes, peace and tranquillity which seemed odd.

He did not flinch when they whipped him; instead, he felt sorry for the boys. He could not understand how anyone could encourage such young boys to become cruel.

And so, he walked through the gates, chest out and his head held high. The bag tied around his waist still had the oja in it.

Igwekala called out to him as they whipped them,

"Obinna, they are going to kill us," he sobbed as he limped and shook with each whip. "They are heartless; even their young ones are heartless."

Obinna looked back at him and spoke reassuringly:

"Igwekala, they are our audience, and this is our stage," he replied, nodded at Igwekala and walked in.

They slammed the gates shut after they had all gone in and the warriors instructed Obinna and his villagers to wait in a straight line.

Obinna seized the opportunity to marvel at the beauty of that village. There were numerous gigantic structures, statues of warriors carved from gold stood tall and were arranged all around the arena's circumference. They built their seats in a circular arrangement, and the rows rose to ninety feet. In the middle of the arena was a podium carved from stone.

Obinna thought that perhaps the arena was a venue for some entertainment or festival.

Numerous activities were going on at the same time. There were cages where they kept wild animals, an area where women cooked; men wrestled for entertainment and bladesmiths made swords.

He saw a group of men with long flowing hair and tribal marks on their faces, holding scrolls and when he listened, it seemed they were teaching a group of young people things about magic and sorcery.

He could hear people playing musical instruments which he was not familiar with and was very interested in seeing what instruments they were.

He could smell the pleasant aroma of herbs and spices which the women were cooking meat with, and it made his mouth water. His stomach rumbled as it had been a while since he had a decent meal.

The people in the arena did not pay too much attention to Obinna and his villagers. They would look at them briefly and carry on with what they were doing.

Obinna heard sounds coming from the upper part of the arena and looked up; he saw hundreds of birds in cages hanging from several corners of the walls. The cage's doors were left open to allow the birds to fly around freely.

So, the people of Tangandoom love animals, food and entertainment, he thought. "Perhaps they are not too different from us," he whispered.

His thoughts were interrupted as he saw some men laying down deer hide on the floor around the podium in the centre of the arena. The fur was decorated with beads and had the symbol of the rising sun painted on it. The men laid it from the podium to an exit that led into a passageway.

The executioner emerged again but this time accompanied by six warriors who all ran towards the exit where they laid the hide.

The warriors knelt at the exit with their heads bowed,

and the executioner flung both his arms in the air and bellowed.

"Rulership is the natural order, the lion rules the jungle, and the sea monster rules the ocean, day rules over the night," he paused, took a deep breath and continued, "Tangandoom, behold the rising sun is here, our king and ruler Gandoom is here."

A prolonged silence followed as Obinna and his villagers were forced to kneel and lower their heads. They were told not to look at the king until he got to the centre of the podium.

And the king, Gandoom emerged from the passageway accompanied by an entourage of warriors and magicians.

Obinna wondered why it was not okay to raise his head and look at the king. He looked at Igwekala from the corner of his eyes and noticed he not only bowed his head but also had his eyes closed as he was afraid.

He could hear drummers tapping on their drums with each step Gandoom took, and it felt as if the earth shook as he walked in.

He began to wonder why he was conforming to their demands. He understood what authority stood for and also honour and respect but was not convinced that he owed the king that, after all, respect is earned and this king was nothing but their tormentor, an evil omen which he hoped will cease to exist. Besides he was curious, he wanted to see the king's face.

So, he raised his head and looked at him as he walked majestically towards the podium at the centre of the arena.

He could see that the king was middle-aged, very handsome and quite tall. His skin looked like polished bronze, and his bright white teeth contrasted his eyes which were red like a burning furnace. He had long flowing dark hair which cascaded down his very muscular shoulders like the waterfalls of *Ugwuani,* which Obinna loved to see as a child. His garment was made from leopard skin, and he wore a lot of ornaments, bracelets and beads which had pendants made from the skulls of animals.

The executioner walked behind Gandoom as he approached the podium while a group of women in the crowd were rolling on the floor with their eyes still closed and singing songs of praise to him.

Obinna could not get his eyes off him. The king looked healthy and very well-groomed. His skin, elegance and gentle strides all added to his grandeur.

But little did Obinna realise that he was doing the unthinkable. Nobody in Tangandoom looked at the king during his procession, at least not until he got to the podium.

It became clear to him that he had done something unusual when Gandoom stopped walking all of a sudden, looked at the floor, slowly raised his head and looked at where he knelt, making eye contact with him.

Obinna and Gandoom stared each other in the eye for what seemed like a minute, but that minute felt very long, it was as if two worlds had collided; a world where respect was a Hobson's choice and another where the options were free and fair.

He made his choice that day; he chose to look at Gandoom and was fully ready to bear the consequences.

Gandoom looked away and whispered into the executioner's ears. He pointed at Obinna and carried on with his procession.

The king stepped on the podium alone and began to speak in the most gentle and eloquent voice which Obinna had ever heard. There was something weirdly relaxing about the way he talked, which could convince anyone listening to pay attention for hours. He was very well-spoken and intelligent, and each sentence was thought through before he spoke.

"Tangandoom, you may now behold your king," he said. "Look, and then look around you," he carried on as Obinna began to look everywhere to understand what Gandoom was trying to say.

"Do you see despair?" the king asked. "These treasures, fountains of cow milk and towers that embrace the stars; was it despair that created them? No, it was you." And the entire crowd cheered and clapped while the king waited for them to become silent again before he continued.

"You are the ones that turned your backs on despair and obeyed; you built these things because you obeyed the rising sun; you obeyed me, and hence these things were made possible for you to enjoy."

The crowd exploded with cheers, the king's executioner nodded his head in affirmation and smiled as he stood watching everyone's response.

"Bring me the treasures that you have acquired from Umuzura, impress me and let me see the gifts you have brought back, which I have not seen before." He spoke as he looked down at the executioner who immediately summoned the warriors to show the king what they brought back.

The executioner bowed and replied,

"Great king, we have brought the best ivory that Umuzura has, rare star apple and *pawpaw* seeds that we will cultivate and grow into huge plantations and these workers will assist us at the cornfields to plough and make ridges for our crops." He gestured at Obinna's villagers.

"We also brought you this gift which I'm sure you will love," the executioner asserted and approached the warrior who held the cage that Udele, the parrot, was kept.

He removed the black cloth covering the cage, reached into it and picked the parrot up by her legs.

"Great king, this is the so-called magical parrot we have heard that delivers prophecies to these people's village," he explained. "They live their lives according to what it tells them."

Gandoom's eyes lit up with excitement when he saw Udele, he reached down, picked up the parrot and raised his arm on which she perched.

"Hmm," he hesitated, carefully observing the bird. "A magical parrot? I like its feathers and colour." Gandoom rubbed Udele's head gently and placed the parrot on the podium.

He began to talk to Udele and Obinna could see that the king liked the bird.

"Tell me something then, my friend, what prophecies have you got for me?" the king joked.

Udele flapped her wings, raised her neck and looked straight at Obinna where he stood with Igwekala and Obinna began to feel sick to his stomach.

He felt chilly as cold sweat trickled down the side of his forehead, and his legs felt numb. It was a similar feeling to what happened to him on that bridge back home at Umuzura, the bridge that had its banks lined by coconut trees, where he saw the distressed crows and the whirlwind before they besieged his village.

He began to lose consciousness while taking deep breaths as he struggled to stand on his feet. All he could hear was Gandoom's voice as it echoed in his head.

"Tangandoom, dance and rejoice now for the whirlwind has blown, and it brings forth tidings of prosperity, gifts and riches!" the king bellowed with both his hands raised towards the sky. "But amidst this abundance, I curse anyone of you who chooses to wine and dine with despair or dishonour, drink from that cup of disobedience and you will surely be put to death; and after the fire of my justice consumes you, ashes and dust you will surely become forever."

And when he said that, Udele spread her wings, squawked loudly and repeated the words, "Prophecy, prophecy."

Obinna's legs gave up, and he fell backwards, it felt as if an unseen force had hit him, but Igwekala caught him as he fell and both men tumbled to the ground as Igwekala's leg had not healed and could not support Obinna's weight.

The arena erupted again with cheers as the king concluded his speech, took Udele with him and was escorted out.

Drummers began to thump loudly on their instruments, dancers and entertainers jumped out from within the crowd and started to cheer and perform.

Igwekala began to cry and held Obinna's head on his lap as they lay.

"*Nna, o ga adi nma,*" he spoke to Obinna in their native language, "You will be okay," he reassured his friend and burst into tears again.

"I am going to miss Umuzura and holding my keys to

the masquerade hut," he lamented and Obinna opened his eyes and smiled while still dazed.

"Well Igwekala, there will probably be a new set of keys for the masquerade hut as I'm sure you have lost the old ones after we got besieged," Obinna responded. "The lock to the masquerade hut will be changed, and you might hold those new keys again when we get back home," he joked.

Igwekala smiled apprehensively but replied:

"That would only happen if these madmen have not already burnt down the masquerade hut."

Obinna replied:

"Igwekala, the spirits of our ancestors are the masquerades, fire consumes only the physical, but if the fire goes to war with spirits, it will lose."

He had not finished speaking when three warriors approached them. One of the men spoke with a raised voice,

"All men, move to the right and women and children to the left."

Obinna held Igwekala's hands as they both got up; he did not want the two of them to be separated.

He looked back to try and find where his beloved Adaure was and saw her among the women who they moved to the left. He nodded at her but did not say a word as he was still forbidden to speak to her.

Adaure made a gesture at Obinna to draw his attention, and when he looked, she pointed at her chest and Obinna, moving her other hand all over her belly as if to tell him that she was pregnant.

Obinna's eyes lit up with excitement. He repeated the gestures Adaure made on his belly to confirm that he understood what she was trying to tell him, and she nodded.

Adaure was pregnant with Obinna's child. The signs were not very apparent as she was two months into the pregnancy.

She had known about it before their village was attacked and decided to keep it secret for a while, but that day, she thought it was best to let him know.

Obinna continued to look back at her as they led the men from the arena into a passageway.

The noise from the arena gradually faded as they walked further in, and all he could hear was the clattering of metal.

*

Igwekala limped alongside him, and Obinna could see that he was shaking all over with fear.

They were all led to a group of men who had metal sticks which they inserted into a big pot that had red hot liquid in it.

The men would lift the metal from the pot and press it against the skin of each person that they approached. The sticks were tattoo devices which left a mark of the rising sun on their chests, and an ointment was rubbed all over the wound to allow it to heal correctly.

They led them from the passageway to wooden cages that had ropes attached to it. The strings were tied around wheels that served as a pulley system, used to lift the cages about 160 feet above the ground. It was in those upper floors that they built their prisons.

Obinna figured out that perhaps they built those prisons there to make it impossible for anyone to escape. Any runaway prisoner would either have to jump to their death or require the cages and pulley lowered for them which he was sure would not happen.

Obinna and Igwekala got on one of the cages accompanied by a warrior. They both felt very dizzy as the men who operated the pulley lifted them.

As the ropes were pulled up, Obinna could see the horizon far away; he loved the scenery and landscape. He closed his eyes and took a deep breath of the fresh air that blew against his cheeks.

"Umuzura, our home is somewhere over there," he murmured, "I believe that someday, we will see her again."

They rolled the cages down each time prisoners were dropped off to carry some more to the upper floors.

"Step out and walk straight to the first chamber on the right," the warrior spoke to Obinna as they let them out of the cage.

Igwekala followed as the warrior led them to their prison's gate, unlocked it and pushed them in.

Obinna observed the room as the warrior left. He could see that a mat had been laid on the floor for them to sleep on and there was a small window to let in some sunshine, but they secured it with iron rods that could barely fit a person's palm hence it was impossible to climb through it. There was also a water pot, a lantern that lit up the room at night, two bowls for them to eat with and a book made from bamboo left on the floor.

Obinna picked up the book, flipped through the pages, and it seemed to be mostly about the king's power, wars he and his people had won, and some pages had instructions on how to be a loyal subject to Gandoom as well as a short history about Tangandoom and their way of life.

Obinna understood the message within the book as Tangandoom and his village, Umuzura spoke the same language, but he quickly put the book down. He was not interested in its contents at all.

He noticed messages had been written all over the walls in the room. He could read some of the notes, and they seemed to be words of pain and agony left by former inmates. He could not understand some of what was written as they used symbols which were unfamiliar to him, but he noticed a particular message written in text that had similar English alphabets as those they used in Umuzura even though it had phonetic symbols he could not correctly interpret and he read the words aloud to himself.

"To find your way out, you must first find your way in, for the keys that you seek are with and within you."

Obinna continued to stare at the message on the wall. He wondered who wrote it and was very worried about what might have happened to the people who were in there before him or where they captured them.

"How are you feeling?" he asked Igwekala who had already laid down and was about to sleep.

"I am exhausted and hungry," Igwekala replied. "My wounded leg is not getting any better, and I will need some medicine for it."

Obinna walked towards him, took his palm and started to massage the area where the joint of his index finger and thumb came together, a technique they used in his village to alleviate pain.

"Igwekala, I would like to tell you something," he said.

"What?" Igwekala whispered, paying little attention to Obinna. "Yes, what would you like to tell me?"

Obinna hesitated for a while, stared at the ground and whispered:

"Adaure is pregnant with my child."

"Really? I mean how, when?" Igwekala stuttered as he tried to jump up, but the pain in his leg forced him to lie down again.

"Obinna, this is great news, right?" Igwekala asked his friend, not sure of exactly how to respond.

"But, here in Tangandoom, will they let Adaure give birth?" Igwekala asked. "How will Gandoom react to it?" he carried on.

"How long have you known about this?"

It seemed Igwekala's questions would never end. He would not let Obinna respond before he threw in another matter.

"She told me today at the arena shortly before we came in here," Obinna whispered.

He lay next to his friend and continued to rub his palm as he spoke, asked him to close his eyes, relax and think of something beautiful like a forest of palm trees or a herd of young antelopes galloping through a large field while it drizzled at sunrise.

Obinna had rubbed his palm for what seemed like hours as they discussed the situation and did not realise when he fell asleep himself.

That day's activities had worn them out, and they both lay next to each other in silence that was disturbed by Igwekala's loud snoring.

*

Obinna felt a gush of wind blow against his face. He opened his eyes, got up and was surprised to see himself holding onto the wooden rails of a bridge. It was that same wooden bridge built over the small river which had its banks lined with coconut trees; the bridge where his late father gave him the oja.

He was dreaming, but it all felt genuine. He heard a faint voice singing from underneath the bridge, looked down and saw that it was Adaure.

She was knee-deep near the riverbank and held a small wooden cup in one hand while she created calm ripples in the water with the other as she sang:

"Love, find me; love, hate me; love, kill me, after all, it is only you; so, love it is still okay."

It was the most beautiful voice Obinna had ever heard. He ran to the edge of the bridge, got off and stepped into the river. He hugged Adaure's big stomach as they both swayed to the song she was singing. He tried to speak to her but could not. He realised his lips were moving, but no sound came out from his mouth, and that frustrated him as he tried harder.

Adaure placed her index finger against his lips to discourage him from talking. She held his cheeks with one hand as she stared into his eyes, beaming with smiles. She dipped her finger in the wooden cup which had some olive oil in it and smeared Obinna's forehead with the oil.

"Don't worry my love; this will take all the stress and pain away."

Both of them felt as if they were alone in the universe and time and space had stood still for their sake.

It was a moment shared by two lovebirds who did not

care about what would happen next. All Obinna cared about was the fact that she was there next to him and he enjoyed every moment of it as they both made ripples with their hands in the river.

The dream did not last very long. Obinna heard a loud squawk overhead, and when they looked up, they saw the parrot, Udele flying past them and repeating "Prophecy, prophecy," as she drifted.

Thunder and lightning struck; day turned to night, and heavy rain followed. His dream had quickly turned to a nightmare, and he felt the need to grab Adaure and run as he began to experience that sick feeling in his stomach, which made him feel dizzy.

They both ran to the edge of the river, drenched from head to toe.

Obinna pulled Adaure to the riverbank, and they both lay side by side, taking deep breathes while he looked up to see if the parrot was still there.

Udele was gone, but the heavy rain continued. Obinna looked at Adaure, and it seemed she had stopped breathing and lay there lifeless.

"Adaure, Adaure!" he called out while sobbing and shaking her in an attempt to resuscitate her to no avail.

*

The rain in his dream continued, but it was interrupted when he suddenly woke up and realised someone had thrown a cup of water in his face in the prison where he was sleeping.

He jumped up to see who it was but had to wipe the water from his face first to see clearly. There was no light coming through the small window in the cell, so he realised they had slept through the evening, and it was dark outside.

A strong smell of burnt charcoal filled the air inside the prison, and that smell was familiar. Obinna heard footsteps approaching from the entrance, and the sounds of the cages as they descended made him realise that someone had been let up into their prison.

Obinna ran to the opposite side of the wall with fear to avoid any contact with the uninvited guest.

Meanwhile, Igwekala was still snoring.

"Who is that?" Obinna asked, scratching the tattoo on his chest as it had started to itch.

The visitor did not respond but turned on a lantern he held so Obinna could see his face. Obinna recognised the wrinkled face, that looked like wet charcoal had been smeared all over it, and the thin film that covered one of his eyeballs. He remembered his encounter with the stranger at Umuzura, on his way to the Udunre festival and knew it was the same older man.

The man placed his lantern on the floor and looked back to ensure nobody followed him in. He brought out an ointment and a clean piece of cloth from a bag he carried, soaked the fabric in the lotion and walked towards Igwekala.

"Get away from him," Obinna snarled. "He is not feeling well."

"I know," the man replied, "and that is why I have brought this medicine, to help him recover."

The man went to where Igwekala was sleeping, held the ointment with both hands as he recited a mantra, walked three times around Igwekala and knelt next to him.

He poured some of the ointment on Igwekala's wound

and wrapped it up with the cloth soaked in the lotion.

Igwekala moved a bit but was too tired to wake up and slept through all that was going on.

"So, you have a lot of questions to ask me, don't you?" the man remarked, as he stood face to face with Obinna.

Igwekala started to convulse where he lay, with his eyes closed and Obinna became very concerned.

"Do not worry," the man chimed in, "the medicine is made from a mixture of dog saliva, venom from the pit viper snake and treated charcoal." He continued to explain, "that is a normal reaction to the potion, he will recover quickly afterwards."

"So, how are you feeling?" the man asked Obinna without making eye contact. Obinna became a bit upset by the question he was asked and interrupted:

"How am I feeling?" he mimicked the stranger's question and voice. "Oh, I feel great," he responded sarcastically. "I could not feel any better.

"Everything we have has been stolen from us," he complained. "We have all been stolen from our lands and brought here." Obinna was full of rage as he confronted the older man and held him by the garment.

"For what purpose?" he asked the man as he shook him violently. "For what purpose?" he sobbed and left the man alone when he realised that perhaps he had spoken to him too harshly.

"I saw you on the way to Udunre festival, I gave you directions, and if I remember, I think I gave you some food or was it nuts?" he said, while still shaking with rage.

"And here you are; I did not realise that you were a spy who worked for the enemy."

The older man looked at Obinna with pity and replied, "Water, not nuts or food," he continued, "you gave me water, and you also helped me carry my bag if I remember," the man declared, "I am very grateful for your help; thank you."

"I cannot understand why you have chosen to repay my kindness with evil," Obinna complained. "Where is your conscience?"

The man did not respond to that but instead put his hand in the bag he carried and brought out a keg of water, calmly walked towards the water pot in Obinna's prison and poured all the water into the container. He proceeded to where Igwekala lay and felt his body temperature with his palm and nodded.

"I have now repaid you, good deed for good deed," he explained. "In return for the water you gave me, there's some in your pot." He carried on, "You carried my bag, my burden, so I have treated your friend, and you do not have to carry him any longer." The man added, "I have been watching you carry him all along the journey.

"Now we are even, and I no longer owe you anything," the older man concluded.

Obinna was not satisfied with his response. He quickly went to the water pot, scooped some water with the cup in his prison cell and gulped the water down as he was very thirsty.

"No," Obinna argued, "you have taken more from me than you have given."

He slowed his speech to enable him to catch his breath. He had drunk the water too quickly, some of it trickled down the wrong part of his throat and made him cough.

"You betrayed us and took away our freedom; nothing you give me will be equal to that which you all have taken from us."

"Well, maybe you are right," the man responded. "There is one more thing I will have to pay you for."

"And what might that be?" Obinna asked angrily. "You are part of the same evil, and I don't think I need your help."

"Directions," the man replied. "You gave me directions to my destination when I first saw you."

Obinna laughed and replied:

"Listen, old man, the only directions I will need right now is how to get my people out of this land which you have brought us into."

"Hmm," the man gasped, "I am not sure I can help you with that." He carefully observed how Obinna would respond to what he had said before speaking again.

"You see, loyalty is important; I pledged allegiance to Gandoom, my king and have been loyal to him ever since."

Igwekala had started to gain consciousness and slowly wriggled where he lay. He opened his eyes with much effort and was surprised to see a stranger talking to Obinna in their prison cell. He lay there trying to figure out if he was dreaming, a part of him wondered if he was already dead and was having an afterlife experience. He did not say a word and just listened to the dialogue.

"Loyalty is part of the fabric of the universe," the man continued. "Night is loyal to the day, and the daytime clouds are loyal to rain; rain bows to the sand which absorbs it and the plants that grow are loyal to all these; cause is also loyal to effect hence one must give way for the other to occur at the appointed time."

"Loyalty?" Obinna refuted. "You call this loyalty?" he exclaimed as he walked around the man in circles.

"This is not loyalty; it is evil; man's inhumanity to his fellow man."

Obinna stopped walking and glared at him. His heart had started beating fast while he spoke,

"You insist that loyalty is part of the fabric of the universe, but what about you and me?" he asked. "Must we hurt each other because we are slaves to loyalty; or cause and effect?"

He encircled the older man again and stopped in front of him, staring him in the eyes.

"If we all die, the universe and loyalty will die with us; cause and effect will cease to have meaning," Obinna concluded.

"Everything becomes nothing when nothing is there to witness everything."

The older man's eyes became fixed with Obinna's as he pondered upon what he had said. He heaved a sigh and replied,

"You want directions to get out from this place?" he asked. "You believe I owe you that, right?"

"It is the right thing to do," Obinna replied.

"The directions you seek are with and all around you; you hold the key, so you just have to look and see it."

Obinna heard what the man said and looked at himself from head to toe. All he had with him were the garments he wore and the oja in that bag hanging around his waist.

He had forgotten entirely about the oja as it felt like a part of his body. He had worn it around his waist for a month.

He looked around and pointed at the message he had read earlier written on the wall.

"Who wrote that message?" he asked the man.

"A former inmate here, he was from the Far East," the man replied.

"And what happened to him?" Obinna asked.

"He was cursed and became mad; he thought a bird was attacking him and even behaved like one; flapping his arms all day, then started scribbling messages all over the walls."

"Then he wrote that particular message; yes, that one you are looking at that says, to find your way out, you must first find your way in, for the keys that you seek are with and within you.

"He placed his forehead on the message for weeks and refused to move, then one day, the warriors came up and found an empty cell.

"That man disappeared without a trace; left no marks; no trail; some even believed he turned into that bird that haunted him and flew away.

"Listen, my time is up here, they will soon roll the cages down, and I have to go." The older man cut off the conversation and handed Obinna some hare meat wrapped in leaves.

"This is your dinner," the man informed him, picked up his lantern and walked away.

"Obinna, who is this?" Igwekala asked.

He had fully woken up and had to understand what was going on.

"Yes, tell us, who you are," Obinna asked the older man as they heard the sounds of the cages being rolled down.

The cage had stopped at their floor; a warrior had dismounted and unlocked the entrance gate to let the man in who turned around to Obinna and Igwekala before he got into the cage and replied.

"My name is Suleiman; I am the king's magician and the king's curse."

*

Obinna staggered back to their mat and offered Igwekala some water and meat which he ate quickly. He carried on, staring at the message on the wall as they ate.

"How long have I been sleeping and who tied this cloth on my leg?" Igwekala asked. "Who was that man, and why did he come in here?"

"That man treated your wounds and also gave us this food; he is a spy for Gandoom; I saw him at our village on my way to the Udunre festival."

"A spy?" Igwekala asked. "But I just heard him say he is a magician; we cannot trust him; please be careful."

"My leg feels a lot better," Igwekala declared, stood up and limped to Obinna. Both men stood side by side staring at the message on the wall, and Igwekala continued:

"I heard what he said about the man who wrote this message."

"Obinna, what are we going to do about Adaure?" he asked. "She is pregnant, and you will have to let someone know sooner than later because it might not be safe for her and the baby if these warriors find out themselves; they might hurt her and the child."

"Igwekala, let me sleep and think about it."

Both men had finished their dinner and Obinna rearranged the mat with Igwekala's permission, laying it closest to the window so they could inhale the fresh air as it blew into their prison cell.

It had become pitch black outside, and hundreds of stars illuminated the skies which Obinna could see as he peeked through their window.

Igwekala had fallen asleep, and Obinna sat there wishing he would have that same dream and see Adaure again. He found it difficult to sleep and even tried to force himself to no avail.

He remembered a ritual he had learned from his late father that helped people relax and sleep faster and decided to try it.

His father taught him that sleep was an angel that rode the winds; if one wished to sleep peacefully, they should clear their mind and be one with the wind, talk to it, feel it and then sleep will glide through and become one with that person.

So Obinna took a deep breath while standing at the window. As the wind blew on his face, he closed his eyes and Spoke to the wind.

"Yes, I understand that all is connected, you embrace us when we breathe in and you become us when we breathe out so you can embrace us again."

He spread himself out on the mat next to his friend and fell asleep.

*

Obinna started dreaming again. The thoughts he held firmly about Adaure influenced his dream, and yet he found himself on that same bridge.

He did not waste much time and ran to the edge of the bridge, hoping that she would be in the river as before, but she was not there.

While he leaned over the bridge to see if she was in the river, a part of him wished that the parrot, Udele would not appear again.

What he experienced was awkward. His subconscious mind knew that he was dreaming, but he had no control over what ensued.

"Are you looking for someone?" a voice echoed behind him.

Obinna froze with fear as he was sure there was nobody on the bridge and echoes are unfamiliar phenomena in that riverbank. He hesitated for a while to turn around but obliged when the voice spoke his native dialect and called him by his name.

"Obinna, my son."

He could not believe what he was hearing. It was his late father.

He still looked the same and had that solemn smile on his face, which Obinna could not quite decipher when he was growing up if it showed happiness or sadness.

Obinna ran to embrace him on the bridge, but his father refused and instructed him to stay where he was.

"Papa, I have missed you," Obinna said as they both stood facing each other.

"I have missed you too, my son, but I do see you every day," his father replied.

"How? Papa, you left me for years."

"No, those stars you see in the skies at night are your ancestors looking down at you," his father responded. "We have been watching you."

"Papa, we have been cursed; Umuzura is in trouble."

His father interrupted him before he could explain all that has happened.

"Who told you that you are cursed?" his father asked.

"Udele, the parrot, delivered the prophecy, King Gandoom besieged Umuzura, and we all are now prisoners in Tangandoom," Obinna responded.

"My son, the fact that the parrot cursed Umuzura does not mean that you are cursed," he clarified and continued, "so, if I tell you that you are going to die, you will believe me just for the mere fact that I said so?"

"No, but it is Udele that said so," Obinna argued, "Udele is special and sacred; she is a magical parrot."

His father shook his head and said:

"No, my son, magic is all around you." And his father disappeared and reappeared behind him on the bridge.

Obinna turned around to see him, and he disappeared.

"You see, everything is magical," his father maintained and appeared in front of Obinna.

"The earth, life and death are all part of that magic," he carried on.

"My son, the dung beetle is cursed by its tiny size, but have you ever wondered how it can lift weights many thousand times its body weight?" he asked Obinna.

"And yet a man barely manages to lift a lamb?" he carried on.

"How is it able to do that?" Obinna asked.

"Because it understood its magic first and then tried," he replied.

"The beetle understands that it does not require a lot of strength to carry its own tiny body, so that leaves it with the magical power to carry everything else; so, the beetle has looked within itself, understood its magic and then turned its curse into a blessing."

Obinna thought about what his father had said for a few seconds. It made sense, but he did not feel convinced as to how all that applied to him or the problem they were facing. He did not understand how all that talk about beetles and magic could help him, and his villagers get out from Tangandoom. Besides, he was perturbed about the possibility of his child being born into captivity.

He hung his head in frustration and responded:

"Papa, I have nothing, no strength or magic and Gandoom's army is too powerful."

He started to breathe fast as he spoke, and his father looked at him with pity and replied.

"Obinna, you have the magic you need to win; you have got it right there now with you, so use it."

Obinna paused when he heard what his father had said. He looked at himself from the neck down to his toes and all he noticed was the oja, in the bag around his waist. His father saw him looking at the flute and told him that it had been a while since he heard him play. He asked Obinna to play him a song once more and reminded him that the oja was all he had and playing that instrument was all he knew how to do so, there was nothing more to lose by trying. He reminded him again that the oja was magical, but he had not experienced its magic because he was looking for solutions in the wrong places.

"Play a song for me, my son, and believe that the rhythm from that magical oja will guide you through the journey you are about to go," his father concluded.

Obinna thought about it and agreed. He missed his father

and wanted to show him once again how good he had become with the instrument; he tried to impress him.

So, he opened the bag, slowly pulled the oja out and began his usual dance routine whenever he played; three steps to the left, three to the right and with both hands raised to the sky he jumped up and down like a warrior.

His father's solemn smile immediately changed when he looked at him; he had a big genuine smile on his face and was gently nodding his head in encouragement.

The oja felt very hot when Obinna held it; strong winds shook the bridge as clouds gathered in the skies above; lightning and thunder followed, and Obinna felt an intense energy trickle through his veins.

He felt removed from the bridge, like an astral being surging through everything and everywhere and could see himself radiating with the cosmos in full view in front of him.

That day, he rode the lightning and thunder like friendly but fiery stallions while his destiny and fate had no choice but to observe and let him have his moment patiently.

A moment that Obinna needed.

The writing on his prison wall began to make more sense. He had finally dared to look within, and in that dream, he found his magic.

Obinna exploded with energy and felt infinite particles of himself bursting through an expanse of nothingness. Far into space and time that was endless.

And it all started to calm down when he got sucked back in. From the depth of the universe, he returned to his physical self.

Everything went silent. It was a silence that was almost

audible.

His father was not there anymore, and he was no longer on the bridge and had woken up gasping for breath in his prison cell where he lay next to Igwekala.

*

It was daybreak when Obinna woke up. Small rays of sunshine had started to stream into his prison cell.

He yawned and stretched himself out, and that woke Igwekala up as well. Obinna felt elated that morning. He thought about his dream for a short while and looked down at his waist to check if his oja was still there and it was. He realised that he had not cleaned it for a while, so he used a part of his garment to wipe the flute, blowing into its holes to get rid of dust and particles. Igwekala turned around where he lay and was surprised to see Obinna cleaning the oja.

"Obinna, who are you planning to entertain?" Igwekala asked. "I have not seen you clean that oja in ages."

"Well, you never know who might want to listen to the tune of the spirits," he replied and placed the oja back in the bag tied around his waist.

Obinna felt the need to laugh that morning. It had been a while since he did so. He thought about something funny to share with Igwekala and remembered Ekwueme, the drunkard in his village and struck up a conversation with Igwekala about him.

"Igwekala, have you ever wondered how Ekwueme is doing in his prison cell?" he asked. "I'm worried about him; you see that old man has not had a drink in months, and I think he might die in there," he joked.

Igwekala burst out laughing and replied:

"If they starve him of his drink long enough, perhaps that might make him so angry that he could break down these walls, trample upon Gandoom's warriors and set all of us free don't you think?"

Both men laughed about it and felt better.

The cages were being rolled up again with warriors in each one going to the different cells where they kept the men, women, children and elderly. It was time to feed the prisoners as it was routine for the warriors to come up twice per day and leave enough food to last each prisoner until they visited again.

Gandoom, the king had earlier decided that they should separate the children from their mothers, remove them from the prisons and keep them in the care of women in Tangandoom who he had assigned that duty. Those women would be their foster parents and have the sole responsibility of raising them and teaching them all they needed to know to integrate into their new environment fully. The king thought that it would be too risky to leave the children in the care of their biological parents as they might influence their mind to start a rebellion against him when they grow.

The king had also decided and instructed the warriors to remove the beautiful maidens who danced at Obinna's village during festivals, from the prisons. He intended to keep them all in his palace where they would be well looked after, groomed and taught royal protocols.

As for the elderly prisoners, Gandoom had given the order to also separate and keep them in different work chambers where they would carry out routine minor tasks like feeding his animals, separating groundnuts from their shells after harvest and attending meetings once a week with his magicians and sorcerers as the king valued the intelligence of the elderly and thought that perhaps his magicians might learn a few things from them which would be valuable to Tangandoom.

The rest would remain in the prisons as the primary source of labour for the king, and the warriors who were on their way up had also come to enact the orders.

Obinna and Igwekala stopped laughing when they heard the cage halt on their floor. They both stood up, waiting for the door to open.

The other cages had started to pick others up from several floors, and the silence was disturbed by the sound of metal clattering.

Someone opened the gate to Obinna's cell, and the king's executioner walked in accompanied by a warrior. Obinna wondered why the executioner had come to their cell himself and did not feel good about his visit that morning.

The executioner poured water into their pot and left some meat for them on the floor hurriedly.

"The king has given an order to bring you to his palace." He informed Obinna. "He would like to see you immediately."

The executioner pushed Obinna into the cage and instructed Igwekala to stay behind.

Igwekala became very worried and wondered why the executioner summoned his friend to see the king. He knew in his heart that something was not quite right, but there was not much he could do but to watch as they led Obinna away.

Obinna got on the cage with the two warriors, and they locked the gate behind them while Igwekala was peeping through the window to see what was happening.

Obinna's cage had been rolled a few feet down when he looked through it and saw another cage which was at the same level as theirs.

Abgara, the old lady who was the native doctor at Obinna's village, was in it with the two young boys known as the purifiers, accompanied by a warrior. She held both boys, one in each arm, but there was a distant look in her eyes, and Obinna thought that perhaps she was not feeling very well.

He continued to look and saw Agbara as she started to hum a song with the boys in the cage. He could not understand the words in the song, but it sounded like a chant Agbara usually hummed during the Udunre festival back at Umuzura whenever she was about to perform her spiritual duties.

Both cages were level and were being rolled down at the same time when he noticed the warrior in Agbara's cage suddenly become confused, fidgeting and later froze as if something had possessed him. The warrior slowly reached out and unlocked the door to the cage as Agbara continued humming her song. The warrior moved aside, leaving the entrance to the enclosure wide open.

It seemed that Agbara and the purifiers had cast a spell on the warrior and Obinna could see that but was not sure what she intended to do.

Agbara looked at Obinna and the executioner from her cage and smiled. She raised both hands, flapped her arms around like a bird while the boys also mimicked what she did as if they were all hypnotised and called out to Obinna.

"This persecution will give you wings, and this is how you and Umuzura shall fly away to freedom."

And she led both boys to the cage's door and jumped off with them.

Obinna's heart skipped a beat. He screamed and rushed to the edge of his cage but could not do much as it was locked. His heart broke when he saw the big smile on the two boy's faces as they jumped with Agbara. He saw them as they fell and knew there was no way they would survive the drop.

He sat down on the cage's floor and sobbed, wondering why Agbara had decided to do what she had just done. She had committed suicide and decided to take the boys along with her.

The spell cast on the warrior in the cage was broken, and he became restless when he realised what had just happened.

Obinna and the executioner had almost gotten to the ground floor when he saw Agbara and the young boy's bodies being wrapped up with pieces of clothing. They dragged them away and disposed of their bodies.

The separation continued as Gandoom requested. Prisoners were rolled down and taken to different chambers.

The executioner instructed the warrior who was with him to stay with Obinna when their cage got to the ground level. He unlocked the door and walked towards the warrior who let Agbara out.

When that warrior saw his executioner, he knelt and lowered his head as if he understood what the outcome of his actions would be.

The executioner drew his sword, placed it behind the warrior's bent neck and pushed down with all his might.

"This is what happens to anyone who disobeys Gandoom," he proclaimed and walked back to get Obinna.

Obinna staggered out of the cage. He had just witnessed

three people's death that morning, and the experience stressed him out, but he was not afraid. He had started to believe rather than worry.

His dream at night had given him hope. Hope which could be false or perhaps fantasy, but he believed in that dream as if it happened in real life.

After all, what is the difference between a dream and reality? he thought. He understood that the mind could not differentiate between the two. For all he cared, their imprisonment and the bad things that have happened to him could all be a dream. He could wake up the next day only to find himself in his mud hut at Umuzura; where it all began, preparing to attend the Udunre festival. But he had decided that even if all that had been happening were a dream, his mind, belief, and perhaps his oja would change the outcome of that particular dream and turn his hopes into reality.

He believed he would win and Umuzura would be free somehow.

*

Obinna and the executioner walked through the arena to get to one of the passageways that led to Gandoom's palace. They both sauntered so Obinna would not fall as they bound his legs with a strong chain.

The executioner looked back at him and slowed down further so he would catch up with his pace. As they walked alongside each other, the executioner began to speak to him.

"What is your name?" the executioner asked, "I do not think I have asked you that before."

Obinna did not reply nor make eye contact.

"There is something not right about you; it seems to me that you have a dark cloud that follows you," the executioner continued.

He paused, looked at the bag around Obinna's waist, which had the oja in it and carried on.

"Speak up when I am talking to you," he warned.

He had become frustrated with Obinna's silence and was not comfortable with being ignored.

Obinna continued looking ahead and replied:

"My name is Obinna. I am a flautist who plays the oja and make people happy, and that is what I do for a living."

"Nonsense," the executioner objected, "I know you, unproductive weaklings, from Umuzura; your senseless fetishes that amount to nothing, I know it all," he scolded.

"You people worship a stupid parrot, indulge in all sorts of petty magical tricks and yet I crushed you all with little to no effort."

He increased his pace and walked in front of Obinna as he was getting upset by the conversation.

"I saw what happened up there when that old woman jumped," he added. "She cast a magical spell on my warrior, didn't she?" he asked. "She is a witch, right?

"My warrior let those prisoners out of the cage," he maintained and slowed down again for Obinna to catch up with him.

"What do you want from me?" Obinna asked him, looking him in the eye this time.

"I felt an unusual force when I encountered you on our way here; I felt demons the day I looked at that your flute," he explained. "I also saw the weird reaction of the winds and the clouds that day I challenged you to a fight."

Obinna did not understand what he meant, but he remembered their previous encounter on the way to Tangandoom. All that which the executioner said happened had gone unnoticed by him.

The executioner grabbed Obinna by the garment, shook him and said,

"You are a magician, aren't you?" he accused. "You were trying to cast a spell on me, right?"

"No, I am not," Obinna disagreed. "My oja is my voice." he stated, "It sings and talks; it will speak to you at the appointed time, and you will have no choice but to listen."

"It does not matter anyway," the executioner blurted. "Your demons will be your demise; the king has summoned you and what I will look forward to listening to is his unavoidable justice."

*

The executioner was greeted at the king's palace by one of his aides at the entrance while Obinna was being groomed by a woman who was preparing him to meet the king. It seemed she was inebriated as she slurred, and her eyes were distantly expressive. The woman poured some oil on her hands and rubbed it on Obinna's hair and later doused him with a fragrance which smelled like freshly picked berries.

She became drawn to the tattoo of the rising sun on Obinna's chest, which had almost healed.

"Oh, so they gave you one of those," she purred and checked if the scar was healing properly by rubbing her fingers all over it.

"Nobody goes to the king looking untidy," she explained

as she gave Obinna and the executioner a final pat.

"The king may see you now."

The executioner walked into the palace first, and Obinna followed.

Obinna felt very small when he walked in. The size of the palace, its statues and beauty all humbled him. He was in awe when he observed the way they decorated the surroundings.

Almost everything in there was made from gold. The doors, windows, floor and even the cutlery were all made with red gold, polished to its most excellent quality.

They decorated the interior in such a way that it looked like a garden. There was an artificial river flowing with liquid gold and golden palm trees grown as if the river supplied its nutrients.

He continued looking around as they waited for the king.

Obinna was very surprised when he saw trees grown upside down in the palace. They arranged the trees in alternating rows to the golden palm trees grown upright. Their roots were growing into the roof, and their stems grew downwards in perfectly straight lines and had holes drilled in them.

He was familiar with farming and methods of crop cultivation but had never really seen plants grown that way.

The tables had enough food to feed an entire village. There were fruits, nuts, meat and lots of wine and he wondered why there was so much food and yet very few people to eat it. He thought it was wasteful.

In another part of the palace, he saw artificial rainbows that they created with light shining through glass chambers filled with water. Some of the water chambers harboured colourful fishes.

Obinna noticed something unusual with the rainbows. It was not the usual type he saw in the skies at Umuzura; the kind that symbolises the wet linen of seven colours, spread out by the gods during rainfall, while the sun serenades it with soft rays. Those rainbows had nine colours when he counted them. He had never seen the two new colours before.

He could hear soft music in the air but did not see anyone playing any instruments. He listened more attentively and realised that the music was coming from the trees growing upside down. The upper sections of the palace had vents that channelled strong winds to blow and sway the plants and each time they moved, their leaves and stems whistled and produced the musical notes he heard.

The entire experience made him marvel at the genius of Gandoom and his people. But that romance was cut short when he saw Gandoom's animals. The smaller ones were allowed to roam freely in the palace while they isolated the large wild ones in cages.

Lions, tigers and hyenas all interacted with each other; rabbits, porcupines and lizards crawled around some parts of the palace, and white doves would occasionally fly from one section of the roof to another.

Beauty suddenly turned to repulsiveness when Obinna looked straight ahead and heard squawks coming from the section of the palace opposite the artificial rainbows. It was Udele, the parrot that delivered the prophecy; one of the king's aides was feeding her.

They had built a bird perch for her and Obinna could see that the parrot was unique to the king as they erected the roost right next to his throne.

The bird became restless as soon as she saw Obinna and the aide tried to no avail to calm her down while feeding her some nuts.

Udele looked at Obinna and went into a squawking frenzy; with wings flapping incessantly and loose feathers flying around, the parrot began to say "Prophecy, prophecy."

Obinna started to feel unwell. His heart beat faster, and his temperature began to rise. He had already become used to that feeling of nausea each time he saw that bird and closed his eyes, wishing that somehow, he would open it again to see that the parrot had gone away.

But his wishes did not come true; instead, it was the king that he saw as he entered the palace. The king's presence seemed to calm Udele down, and her squawking and flapping ceased as soon as he walked in.

Slowly and gracefully, Gandoom walked in with six warriors and a few aides.

"Kneel and lower your heads for the rising sun is now in our midst," the executioner commanded.

He forced Obinna to his knees, and everyone in the palace followed suit.

They escorted Gandoom to his throne, which was also made of gold, and the warriors and aides with him knelt with their heads lowered as he sat down.

"You may all rise now," Gandoom said with his usual gentle voice and summoned one of the aides to bring Udele, the parrot to him.

The parrot was picked up from her perch and handed to him, and he smiled while caressing and admiring her.

Amongst the king's aides was Suleiman, the older man that visited Obinna in his prison cell.

Obinna could see that they had not groomed him at all. He still looked very unkempt, and his face had the dark charcoal marks.

Gandoom handed the parrot back to his aide and began to speak to Obinna.

"Worker," he called Obinna, "I understand that your village does not have a king, am I right?" he asked.

"No, we do not," Obinna replied. "We have elders that make the decisions after they cast votes during our village meetings."

"So, these elders you speak of are like kings who do not have any power," Gandoom suggested.

"The power lies with the people; the elders do not force Umuzura to accept their decisions," Obinna responded. "After they cast votes, the people have the right to accept or reject the decisions they have made."

"In that case, the elders do not have any useful purpose as it is the people who rule your village," Gandoom argued and requested an aide to pass him some *kola* nuts which he received, dipped in a spicy sauce and ate.

"Power, law and order are inevitable for a village or kingdom to function properly," he said while chewing the kola nut. "Nobody has power in your village; hence, there are no strong laws nor serious repercussions for breaking them, and that affects the order and outcome of all things."

Obinna remained silent, listening attentively to what the king was saying.

"The powerless elders in your village made the wrong decisions regarding your security and that was why you were all easily defeated by my warriors."

"There is no honour in war; Umuzura has never fought a

war in her history," Obinna argued. "It is their decisions; all our decisions, that helps us wake up when the cockerel crows in the morning and enjoy the simple things of life, which helps us go to bed at night, singing songs to the moon and stars, because we know we will wake up again the next day."

"No," the king objected, "you only live once, so why should you choose to live an ordinary life when you can have it all?" he asked. "Here in Tangandoom, I am the beginning and the end; power is mine, and we have laws; it is my laws that have created all these wonders and abundance that you see," he maintained as he looked around the palace with a smile on his face.

"My power sustains this beauty and order which you see, and anybody who chooses to disobey or threaten that rule will undoubtedly face the consequences."

The executioner had become restless as the conversation carried on between Gandoom and Obinna. He felt jealous because the king spoke to Obinna reasonably, which he thought was abnormal. He believed a prisoner or worker did not deserve all that time and privilege.

Obinna could see him from the corner of his eyes that he was fidgeting with his sword and pacing around.

"Is everything okay?" Gandoom asked the executioner and requested his aide to bring some more *kola* nuts and sauce.

The king also had noticed how restless he had become.

"Yes, the rising sun," he replied, "I am greatly honoured to be in your presence and to serve you," and the king nodded with satisfaction.

Gandoom slowly stood up from his throne, walked a few steps forward, and his aides all moved closer too. He stood tall with his chest out, and neck slightly raised and began to speak again.

Udele, the parrot spread her wings on the bird perch and also raised her neck when the king stood up.

"Yesterday, during my procession at the arena, you were told not to look me in the eye, but you chose to disobey," the king stated.

The smile and calmness on the king's face had gone, and Obinna could see that he had a solemn demeanour as he spoke.

"You made that choice to disobey; is disobedience and discord all that you live for?" the king asked.

"No," Obinna replied, "love is what I live for; to live is to love."

Gandoom looked up towards the roof in the palace, smiled, nodded and responded.

"You are right," he slowly recited, "to live is to love," and looked down towards Obinna with fire and hate in his eyes.

"But to die is to disobey Gandoom!" the king bellowed. "Prisoner, you are now sentenced to death; you will be publicly executed at the arena in three months during the dry season festival."

Udele, the parrot spread her wings on the perch after Gandoom gave Obinna his verdict, flapped it and flew away towards the roof screaming, "Prophecy, prophecy," as she flew.

The verdict broke Obinna's heart when he heard it. He was not afraid but distraught about his unborn child, his villagers and his beloved, Adaure.

He could see Suleiman looking at him. He was smiling,

and Obinna wondered why. The executioner was pleased with the verdict and had stopped fidgeting when the king got up, informed his aides to escort him out as the meeting had ended.

Gandoom and his aides left the room first, and the executioner forcefully pushed Obinna towards the exit.

The woman who groomed Obinna when he arrived reached out and caressed Obinna's hand as they walked past her. She still seemed drunk.

"Do not worry gorgeous," she purred, "death is inevitable; we will all go there someday."

The executioner pushed Obinna from behind, he did not like the fact that the woman was speaking to him, but she continued talking as they walked.

"You will not feel the pain much, their sword is going to severe your neck quickly, and when you open your eyes again on the other side, it will be all over."

∗

They had separated all the prisoners when Obinna was rolled back up to his cell. The maidens, including Adaure, had been taken into Gandoom's palace, they kept the children under the care of their foster parents, and the elders had been moved to their menial work chambers as Gandoom instructed.

Ekwueme, the elder who was always drunk in Umuzura, had refused to be separated and put with the rest of the elders. He had asked the soldiers to beg Gandoom to leave him in the prisons so he could work with the younger prisoners. He felt he was being insulted by the fact that they thought he was old and deserved only menial jobs. He wanted to participate in hard labour like the rest.

Gandoom granted him that request as he thought that after all, Tangandoom had nothing to lose if he had chosen to do hard labour himself.

Obinna did not speak the entire evening in his cell, which bothered Igwekala. He just sat near the window staring through its opening, at the light that shone through. He would occasionally stand up, remove the oja from the bag around his waist and stare at it without saying a word or blow into it.

He would stand up, walk towards the message written on their prison wall, stare again, heave a sigh and walk back to his corner near the window.

Igwekala just sat there watching what he was doing. He would not take his eyes off him even for a second. He knew there was something wrong as Obinna had refused to discuss the king's verdict with him.

His patience ran out when Obinna stood up again, picked up some leftover food from his plate with his palm and stretched his hand through the window after he murmured a few words which were not audible. It seemed he was trying to feed some birds and surely, he was, as Igwekala saw a few birds outside their window perched on Obinna's palm, picking up the food he gave them.

"Obinna, what is going on with you?" Igwekala asked and walked over to him.

Obinna did not respond. He continued to feed the birds and stare outside through the window.

"Are you going to tell me what happened at the palace?" he asked. "You are acting very strange."

Obinna removed his hands from the window, wiped the

crumbs of food in his palm against his garment and walked away towards the message on the wall and Igwekala followed him.

"Obinna, please talk to me," he pleaded. "What happened at the palace? Why are you silent and why are you feeding birds through the window?"

Obinna sighed while still looking at that writing on the wall and replied.

"The bird is responsible for our curse; all that is happening to us is because of a parrot's prophecy; I am giving them love in return and showing them that we are not angry; that we care."

"Okay, I understand," Igwekala agreed, "but what happened at the palace?" he asked again.

"The whirlwind blew, and it has scattered hope across the hills and valleys; the fire of the king's justice has burned me, only for my beloved Adaure to pick up the ashes and dust for eternity!" Obinna cried.

"Obinna, you are speaking with parables," Igwekala interrupted. "What exactly did Gandoom say or do to you?"

Obinna walked away from the wall and stood in front of Igwekala; both men looked at each other in the eye.

"Igwekala? I want to ask you a question," he said.

"Yes, ask me," Igwekala replied.

"Would you say I am truly your friend in all these years?" Obinna asked.

"If I said you were not, I have cursed the day I was born," he replied.

"And would you hold unto hope like you have held those keys for years to the masquerade huts at Umuzura?" Obinna asked again.

"You have my word; I would," he responded, even though he did not fully understand what Obinna was saying.

"I looked Gandoom in the eye during his procession, and it is forbidden; he has sentenced me to be put to death in three months during their dry season festival."

Igwekala went silent for a while but showed no emotion and later replied.

"I was your burden throughout our journey here; you carried me and refused to let me die, so tell me now, what do you want us to do Obinna?"

"I will break the parrot's curse and free Umuzura; I will go to war with Gandoom, and I will need you by my side to do so," Obinna concluded.

Igwekala did not bother to ask him how he was going to achieve that. Both men were deeply troubled by everything happening. In his mind, he had already accepted Obinna's death sentence as if it was his too. He had made up his mind there that he would be willing to die with his friend. Their destinies became bound to each other from then on, even though he was a bit afraid. He was scared of pain; he did not like how the pain felt as his injured leg that had not healed wholly reminded him of it, and he still had a little limp. But Igwekala thought that the pain that awaited them could be different. It could be the type felt by an entire village; the make or break type.

Umuzura's destiny would depend upon that pain.

*

Two months had already passed, and the rainy season had begun to give way to the dry winds that blow sand from the deserts in the northern hemisphere. The rain had become scarce and unpredictable, and Gandoom had given the order to utilise the prisoners to the fullest to work in the cornfields.

Farming in Tangandoom during the dry season was very strenuous, and the prisoners had to work extremely hard to ensure that food would not be in short supply. Gandoom had entrusted that duty to a group of men and women he referred to as "Planners." Their role in Tangandoom was to plan strategies which the prisoners would use to farm, organise and designate duties to them whenever they went out to the fields to work daily. The planners would instruct the prisoners on how to clear and till the land, and also made them build water reservoirs and canals uphill towards the north of the fields, which served as the source of irrigation used to channel the water through their ridges of crops. They showed the prisoners the appropriate way to plant the crops and nurture them.

Those planners were not just there to guide the prisoners as their name suggested. They were brutal and heartless. They believed that lazy people should not be allowed to live and would not hesitate to take the life of any prisoner who was not working hard enough.

Obinna would keep a record of each of his villagers who had died out there each week they went out to work. He would build them a little tombstone with sand and leaves in the fields and write their name on his prison wall with palm oil from his food whenever they returned.

He filled an entire part of his prison's wall with the names of dead people, and he and Igwekala would offer 'Passing over rituals' for the dead ones in their prison cell as they usually would have done back home at Umuzura.

Ekwueme, the drunkard did not like those planners at all. He referred to them as murderers and would always argue with them regarding duties that they have assigned to him. The fact that he was old and temperamental was perhaps the only reason they spared him; besides, as he was very short, the planners usually laughed at him daily as he worked. They saw him as a working clown and kept him there for their entertainment.

Sometimes they would get him drunk on purpose and make him work while inebriated just for the fun of it, but when he sobered up, he would turn to Obinna with explanations and what he thought about them.

"Those bastards are laughing and pointing their crooked finger at me, but they do not realise that the rest of their fingers are pointing back at them while they do so," he would snarl.

Igwekala's injured leg had fully healed, but the wound had damaged a nerve which gave him a slight limp whenever he walked. He had become used to limping and had started to forget that there was a time he walked without one.

Obinna and the rest of the young prisoners had to be rolled down in the cages, to get to the fields then they had to pass through the arena as well as the main gates, and the warriors would escort and leave them with the planners each morning.

Each time Obinna passed through the arena, his heart would skip a beat because he knew it would be where his execution would take place. Sometimes he would feel like shedding a tear but refused to do so.

Igwekala would always reassure him when they passed through and say:

"Do not worry; this is not where you will die; it is where you will live."

They would work till sunset when the warriors would pick them up again and take them back to their cells.

*

It was the last day of the week, the sun had set, and the planners had instructed the prisoners to tidy up their work for the day.

Obinna and Igwekala walked towards the canal to wash the tools they used to work while the other prisoners were still rounding up their work.

Both of them worked a bit quicker than the rest who did not have as much motivation and enthusiasm.

Igwekala had mapped the entire fields and counted the number of planners and warriors who Gandoom had. He had also taken note of all entrance and exit routes through the arena and had done that to help Obinna as he had made up his mind that he would plan a prison break with his friend. He knew that attempting that would fail because they were greatly outnumbered. Not only were Gandoom's soldiers powerful, but he also had archers who were highly skilled in using bows and arrows as well as horsemen; hence, they would lose a battle on or even above ground. Besides, the king had magicians who used sorcery to manipulate physical elements to punish an enemy. They could set someone ablaze with mere spoken words, suffocate an enemy using esoteric, magical incantations and even induce trauma to such an extent that the enemy would bleed from the nose and mouth till they collapsed and died.

Both men had reached the canal before the rest. Igwekala limped hurriedly towards Obinna to speak to him after they had laid their tools on the ground.

"Obinna, it is only a month left before your execution, and we have to come up with a plan quickly," he whispered.

Obinna continued washing his tools in the water and whispered in response:

"It has approached quickly, hasn't it?"

"But seriously you do not have much time left," he maintained. "I think we need to escape from these prisons, but I do not know how."

"Neither do I," Obinna replied and walked away to lay their tools in the sun.

Igwekala followed him hurriedly, not satisfied with why he seemed not to be bothered by what he was telling him.

"We need to find an insider who can help us," Igwekala suggested. "We might be able to convince Suleiman, the king's magician, to help us escape; he seems to be the only reasonable one amongst them."

Obinna objected and replied:

"Suleiman owes a duty to his king; I do not think he will agree to do so."

"Okay, what about Adaure?" Igwekala asked. "She lives in the palace now with the maidens, we could find a way to get her to seduce Gandoom and poison him in his sleep."

Obinna stopped what he was doing and glared at Igwekala from the corner of his eyes. He did not quite like that suggestion but smiled and said:

"Don't be ridiculous, Igwekala."

"But we can't just do nothing; we have to find a way to stop this execution and get out of here," he pleaded. "I am the

106

only one making the suggestions; okay, what do you suggest we do then?" he asked, "I am not going to watch in silence and let you get killed."

Obinna became moved by his friend's concern and replied:

"I am going to find a solution before then."

The rest of the prisoners had finished their tasks and were arriving at the canal in groups to wash their tools.

Obinna and Igwekala had already left the canal and were on their way to meet the warriors and planners when Igwekala brought something to his attention. Amidst the warriors was Suleiman, the king's magician talking to one of the planners.

"Look, Suleiman is over there." He showed Obinna. "This is the best opportunity for us to talk to him; otherwise, we might never see him again."

Obinna agreed, and both men walked towards him without making it very obvious to the rest of the planners and warriors. When they got to a reasonable distance, Suleiman turned around and walked towards them instead, and both men were surprised and stood still.

He walked to Obinna and said:

"Yes, you wanted to see me, right?" He spoke as if he had read their minds and already knew what they had been discussing.

"Go back to the prisons; I will be there tonight to talk to you," he informed Obinna.

Igwekala was elated by Suleiman's response.

"He is willing to talk to us; Obinna this is very good," he rejoiced with a smile on his face but ensuring nobody around could see his reactions.

The warriors and planners rounded the prisoners up, and they were all taken back through the fields and the arena, into the cages and rolled up to their respective cells.

Obinna stayed up with Igwekala, listening attentively for the sounds of the cages when they would be rolled up. They hoped Suleiman would keep his promise and turn up.

Igwekala became impatient pacing around the prison from one corner to the other while Obinna went to where he kept the oja and began to wipe it again, blowing its holes and making sure it was not blocked.

"I do not think that man will come; he is as untrustworthy as the rest of them," Igwekala complained.

"He will come," Obinna calmly told him.

And surely, Suleiman kept his word and turned up as he said. It was Igwekala who first heard the cages being rolled up and limped over to Obinna where he stood looking at the message on the wall.

"Obinna, I think Suleiman is coming; I can hear the cages, I can hear it," he repeated with excitement.

The cage got to their floor, and Suleiman stepped out unescorted. He unlocked the entrance, went to Igwekala with an ointment in a bottle and asked him to sit down which he did. He rubbed the lotion on Igwekala's injured leg and massaged it a bit.

"The medicine worked, but I see that the puncture which caused the wound went in too deep," Suleiman explained. "You will have to learn how to walk with that leg again like a child."

Igwekala was not particularly interested in his leg at that time. He wanted Obinna to go straight to the point and discuss the possibility of their escape from that prison.

Before he or Obinna could say anything, Suleiman spoke:

"You have only a month left before they execute you," he reminded Obinna. "So, is there anything you would like me to do for you?"

Obinna walked away from the wall, came over and sat with him.

"I would like you to send a message to a woman whose name is Adaure; she is the love of my life, and she is pregnant with my child," he pleaded. "She is one of the maidens who were removed and kept at the king's palace," Obinna carried on.

"I want you to tell her about my execution; tell her that no matter what happens, she will have to be strong and look after our child."

"I have already told her," Suleiman replied. "I was with her today at the palace before I came here; she knows everything."

Obinna interrupted, "But how is that possible?" he asked, "I have never discussed her with you before, so how did you know?"

Suleiman smiled and replied, "Both of you come with me."

He stood up and led Obinna and Igwekala to their water pot in the room and told them to look into the water.

"It is possible with magic; firstly, you must understand and believe in the elements; wind, fire, earth and water."

A small gust of air blew in through the window of the prison, the lantern in their room flickered twice on its own and glowed brightly, and they felt the walls vibrate a bit when Suleiman spoke, and he continued, stirring the water in the pot with his fingers while they watched.

"Water soothes, it satiates; it can cause turbulence if provoked, but it is also a mirror for the eyes that dares to see," Suleiman explained.

Obinna saw an image of himself and Igwekala in the water inside the pot as soon as Suleiman removed his hands. He saw everything as it happened when they discussed Adaure's pregnancy while he was massaging Igwekala's palm to ease the pain in his leg.

Igwekala's mouth dropped with fear. He was shocked to see himself and Obinna in the reflection in the water and wanted to run away, but Suleiman patted him on the shoulder and reassured him.

"There is no need to fear; your friend needs to see this because it is his destiny." He told Igwekala.

"I have a message from Adaure for you," he told Obinna. "She said I should remind you of her love and that she has refused to stay on this earth alone," he continued. "She said that where the warrior's swords will send you, she will go with your son happily to spend eternity."

Tears had started to run down Obinna's eyes, and Igwekala was heartbroken as he watched and listened.

Suleiman brought out a small bottle of olive oil he had in a pouch, dipped his finger in it and smeared some on Obinna's forehead and continued.

"But she also said that this her oil would soothe your pain and as for pleasure, only time would tell." Suleiman said.

The three men in the room could hear the sound of the cages faintly as it was being rolled up. It was time for Suleiman to leave.

Obinna wished he would stay a bit longer but understood that they had no choice but to let him go.

Suleiman stretched his hands, placed them on Obinna's cheeks and stared very deeply into his eyes. As he ran his fingers gently down Obinna's neck and shoulders, Obinna had an intense flashback.

He remembered the same scenario with Suleiman months back when they met on his way to the Udunre festival; when he gave him directions and water and offered to carry his bag.

On this occasion, Obinna reached out as well, touched Suleiman's face with both hands and stared deeply into his eyes that had a thin white film that covered it.

He saw Adaure's face in Suleiman's eyeball, smiling back at him, and her face quickly disappeared. He also saw himself on a hill, with the oja in his hand raised towards the sky and could see Gandoom's warriors at the bottom. Light rays from the sun shone through and illuminated the oja, followed by lightning which struck through the flute and shook the ground. When he looked down again, Gandoom's warriors were gone; it seemed the earth opened, and they all fell in.

"I have now served my purpose in your life," Suleiman said. "I have found my magic, now go and find yours," he concluded and walked away from Obinna towards the entrance for the gates to open.

The cage stopped at their floor, they opened the gate, and a warrior stepped out to pick Suleiman up, but when Igwekala and Obinna looked at who came to get Suleiman, something did not feel quite right.

It was the executioner.

He stepped into the prison cell with authority and scanned the room with suspicion but did not say a word. He greeted Suleiman and ushered him into the cage, looked at Obinna once again and left.

*

It had become very dark outside, and the sound of cuckoo birds disturbed the silence, while strong winds made clattering sounds as they blew against a door left open in a passageway that led to Gandoom's palace.

The executioner refused to go back to his chamber and followed Suleiman back to his for questioning. He had become very suspicious of his activities and wanted to satisfy his curiosity.

Suleiman did not say much and just walked alongside him as they both proceeded down a long corridor in the palace.

They both turned right towards the quarters where Suleiman, the aides and some warriors stayed, and Suleiman turned to the executioner and asked him a question.

"What is it that you seek and why are you following me home?"

"I am Gandoom's executioner, and by the power entrusted upon me by the king, I demand answers," he asserted.

Suleiman gently opened the door to his chamber, and the executioner followed him in without asking for permission to enter.

The executioner began to walk around Suleiman in circles like a soldier who was performing a drill with his subordinates and continued to ask questions.

"Something does not add up," the executioner emphasised. "Firstly, for some reason, you have visited those two prisoners more often in the last few days than anyone else here in Tangandoom," he accused. "Then I saw you talking to one of them at the canal, whispering something to him," he continued, with his hands crossed at the back and walking from one part of the room to the other.

Suleiman did not react but walked away and began to set the table for his dinner.

"Then, to add insult to injury, you revisit them tonight; past their dinner time," he argued. "Suleiman, you surely did not go there to give them dinner because you are not the one designated to do so tonight and it was way past the time for the prisoners to eat."

The executioner clutched his sword but did not draw it from its sheath. He was agitated but seemed to still have a bit of respect for Suleiman's position as the king's magician.

He let go of his sword and walked over to him, taking deep breaths as he spoke.

"So, I ask you now, for the sake of honour and respect for Gandoom; Is there something going on that I need to know?"

Suleiman did not respond immediately but gently removed the pouch he had with him from his garment and placed it on top of his dinner table, pulled out a chair from underneath the table and sat down. He looked at the executioner who stood there, waiting for his response and replied.

"Executioner, do not always be quick to draw your sword; a sword only knows how to react and cannot think or feel."

The executioner went straight to the pouch that Suleiman placed on the table, picked it up, and when he emptied its contents, he found the olive oil bottle that Adaure had given him for Obinna. He smelled the bottle first and later inserted his index finger into it and rubbed the finger against his thumb to feel the texture of the oil.

"This is olive oil," he explained. "You and I both know that olive oil is not popular here in Tangandoom; we use palm and coconut oil."

The executioner went silent for a while to give it a good thought and continued:

"So that means that this oil is foreign and not from our lands. I will henceforth seize it as it is customary that Gandoom must see and give his approval first before it is allowed here in Tangandoom."

Suleiman did not try to explain, so the executioner decided to leave and took the bottle with him.

"Goodnight Suleiman!" he bellowed, stormed out and slammed the door shut.

*

The executioner immediately sent a message to Gandoom through one of his aides. He informed the king that he would like to discuss some things with him regarding Tangandoom's security to which the king obliged and requested him to come to his palace the following day, in the afternoon.

Meanwhile, in the king's palace, it was customary for the maidens to dress up, tidy the surroundings and set up tables with food and wine before the king arrived for such meetings.

Adaure had fully integrated with the rest of them. Her pregnancy had become very obvious as she was almost due but refused to tell anyone who the father of her expected child was. She had lied to the executioner that the father of the child died when the warriors besieged Umuzura and Gandoom allowed her to stay at the palace with the pregnancy.

Gandoom had taken a particular liking to her because she was the most beautiful amongst the maidens at the palace, and he had heard her sing once and fell in love with her voice.

The executioner had his doubts about Adaure's explanation regarding her pregnancy. He knew that she and Obinna were emotionally connected but could not prove it. He was not comfortable with the king's decision to keep her in the palace but could not do anything about it as the king had allowed her to stay.

That afternoon, he hurriedly prepared and got to the palace and was greeted at the entrance by the king's aide. Before he got in, he was groomed as usual by the woman at the door. She rubbed his hair with her palms and brushed the dust off his clothing.

"You came alone today," she purred as usual with her eyes rolling all over the executioner from head to toe. "Where is the other one?" she asked, referring to Obinna.

The executioner brushed past her and did not reply and walked into the palace when an aide informed him that Gandoom was ready to see him.

He went into the palace, knelt with his head bowed and

greeted the king.

"Rising Sun, it is a great honour to be in your presence," he said.

"Executioner, you may rise; Tangandoom values and appreciates your service," the king replied. "Why have you summoned this meeting today?"

"My king, I have served you for years and fought wars for Tangandoom; should I ever stand aside and watch your enemies plot your downfall, let my head roll," he reassured.

The king nodded and smiled with satisfaction at what he had said, and the executioner continued.

"Our enemies tremble at the mere mention of your name; they are loyal, and they know that it is impossible to penetrate our stronghold."

The king reached out and asked his aide for some wine in a cup which he passed over to him.

"Excellent," the king gently said as he sipped the wine.

"But great King, there is an enemy that is yet to be known by you; one which is like a worm eating us out from inside," the executioner warned.

Gandoom stopped drinking the wine and handed it back to his aide. What the executioner said had captured his attention. He sat upright, clenched his hands over his lower abdomen and began to think about what his executioner told him.

"This enemy is a traitor within our midst; gradually plotting your downfall and must be stopped by all means necessary," the executioner advised.

Gandoom stood up from throne and ordered everyone in the palace to leave the room immediately, and they quickly obliged. He asked the executioner to come closer so he could hear him properly without having to raise his voice. He wanted to speak to him privately.

"Executioner, before you speak, you do know that lying to Gandoom bears serious consequences, right?" he reminded him.

"Yes, Rising Sun; I know," the executioner responded. "Your magician Suleiman is not to be trusted; he is a traitor," the executioner informed the king.

Gandoom was shocked when he heard what the executioner said. His facial expression remained calm, and he replied.

"Suleiman?" the king asked. "Impossible; what evidence have you got to prove your allegations?" he asked the executioner.

"I have been watching him for a while now," the executioner replied. "Suleiman visits two of the prisoners in secret and yesterday he sneaked into their prison to discuss something with them."

Gandoom stood up from his throne and walked a few steps away from the executioner. He turned around and replied.

"Which of the prisoners are you referring to?"

"The one who you sentenced to death for disobedience and his friend; the one that limps," the executioner responded.

"Bring the two prisoners and Suleiman now to me." Gandoom sat down and ordered, "I would like to speak to them."

The executioner immediately acted upon the king's request and walked out of the room to bring his warriors back. He informed three of them when they came in to go and bring Suleiman, Obinna and Igwekala as the king instructed.

The three men were later brought in and ordered by the executioner to kneel, bow and greet Gandoom.

Obinna had his oja tied around his waist as usual, and Igwekala limped into the palace with him alongside Suleiman.

They knelt and greeted the king as instructed.

Obinna noticed as they stood up that Suleiman had washed, changed his garment and looked quite different. He seemed unusually well-dressed, and he saw that he had wiped off all the charcoal marks on his face.

It was the first time Obinna had seen him that way, and he wondered why Suleiman looked unusually happy that day.

The three of them stood next to one another facing the king and listening attentively.

Gandoom asked the executioner to speak while he listened.

"Rising Sun, these are the prisoners that Suleiman has been visiting and sharing secrets with," he accused, pointing at Obinna and Igwekala.

"What secret has Suleiman been sharing with them?" Gandoom asked.

"I do not know," the executioner replied, "but I am sure there is something suspicious about his visits to their prison," he argued.

"He has broken your law; you have given the order that under no circumstances should anyone from Tangandoom have any personal relations with a prisoner here that the king is not made aware of," the executioner reminded Gandoom. "But Suleiman has broken that law by visiting them without authorisation; these prisoners are his friends."

The king glared at the three men and calmly spoke to Suleiman.

"Suleiman, speak for yourself," the king requested. "Are these allegations true?"

Suleiman walked away from Obinna and Igwekala, took a few steps towards the king and replied.

"Yes, Rising Sun; I visited them on my own, and yes, I can say that they are now my friends."

Igwekala became very nervous when Suleiman gave his response. He felt that he was putting all of them at risk and that he should have lied.

The king went silent for a while and began to speak again.

"Why? Suleiman," he asked. "For what purpose did you visit and befriend these prisoners?"

"I visited and befriended them because it is his destiny as well as mine," Suleiman responded, pointing towards Obinna as he spoke.

The king spoke to the executioner and asked:

"Executioner, do you have anything else to say?" he queried. "Have you got more evidence before I pass judgement?"

The executioner informed the king that he had more evidence and asked him for permission for his men to go and search Adaure's room before he continued.

"Rising Sun," the executioner acknowledged the king, "I will instruct my warriors to go and search the pregnant lady's room for some evidence because I am aware that Suleiman visited her as well; I need to prove something to you."

The king agreed, and the executioner walked over to his

men and whispered some instructions to them. He told them exactly what to look for and also bring her along with them.

The three warriors left the palace and ransacked Adaure's room. They returned later with Adaure and gave the executioner what they had found.

Obinna became nervous when he saw Adaure walk in. He saw how big her belly was and from his calculations, knew that her child would be born anytime soon. They both looked at each other and Obinna noticed tears trickling down her eyes. They had not seen each other for a while, and he missed her. He was tempted to hug her but remained calm so the king would not know he knew who she was.

The executioner continued with his allegations. He reached into his garment and brought out the olive oil bottle he had earlier seized from Suleiman and showed the king.

"Rising Sun, I seized this bottle from Suleiman yesterday when I followed him home. He took it with him to visit these prisoners."

The executioner walked forward and handed Gandoom the bottle and carried on.

"It contains olive oil, and you and I know that we do not grow olive trees in Tangandoom, and we do not use the oil from it; we use palm and coconut oil."

Gandoom smelled the oil in the bottle, dipped his finger in it and rubbed it against his thumb to feel the texture. He instructed one of the warriors to bring an aide into the room, and when the aide came in, the king gave him the bottle to confirm what was in it.

"Surely, this is olive oil, Rising Sun," the aide confirmed, and the king told him to leave the palace again so he could continue with the meeting.

"So, I wondered where Suleiman got this oil from," the executioner added. "And to my surprise, look at what my warriors have found after they searched her room now," he accused Adaure and held the bottle the warriors found in her room up so the king could see.

"Olive oil," he proudly declared. "The same oil that Suleiman took to these prisoners; this woman gave him the oil, so that means that all of them know each other."

Gandoom went silent again to think everything through and spoke to Suleiman.

"Suleiman, what is this I am hearing?" he asked. "Why have you chosen to betray your king and a village that has treated you so well?"

"Tangandoom has treated me well," Suleiman agreed. "But how has our village treated its neighbours?" he asked. "They have felt nothing but cruelty and violence."

Gandoom became uncomfortable with Suleiman's response. He began to rub his chin and shake his knees restlessly where he sat but continued to listen as Suleiman carried on.

"Rising Sun, this village has changed," Suleiman lamented. "It has become evil and cruel, and I have watched it change," he maintained. "Things were not this way before."

Gandoom became upset, stood up from his throne and replied,

"Suleiman, do not ridicule my authority; how dare you write off my achievements and power with such disdain?"

The executioner drew his sword as he noticed that the king was upset. He was ready to use it and protect him or carry out orders if instructed to do so.

"Life is not all about authority and power," Suleiman interrupted, "the kings before you had authority and power too, but they also understood the true meaning of magic and how it works alongside the universe, to maintain its balance and sustain the common good."

"Did you say common good?" the king asked. "Universal balance?" he further queried, "Suleiman, let me explain something I know about the universe to you and also about good and evil."

He asked the executioner to bring everyone back into the palace before he continued and the executioner walked to the entrance, ordered everyone who the king had earlier requested to wait outside the room to come back, and they did.

The king requested all his aides, the maidens, including the executioner and his warriors to kneel before him, and he spoke firmly to Suleiman.

"You see, in the universe, everything lives off another; there are many things, like the lion and the lamb; the lamb eats grass, but the lion kills the lamb because he also must eat."

The king stepped forward, began to walk around with his hands crossed at the back while speaking.

"To the lamb, the lion is evil but also, to the grass, the lamb is as evil as the lion."

He paused, stood still and looked around his palace before proceeding.

"So, who then is evil? Remember, they all have to eat and also, who gets to define what evil is?"

He stopped in front of Suleiman and continued:

"It is clear to me that you do not understand how the

universe works and you see that which is necessary as that which is evil; my question to you now is who would you rather be, the lion, the lamb or the grass?"

Suleiman slowly replied:

"I do not have to be any of them; I would rather be the earth, the soil, cursed to swallow dead bodies but still spreads out its arms to receive the warm embrace of the grass, lion and lamb's carcass when they die, reminding the universe that it is not a venue for a duel amongst the living; that through its magic, it will give them back as a renewed form of life."

"Nonsense, Suleiman," the king interrupted. "One must live and adapt to that which is necessary for survival in their universe; Tangandoom is our universe, and here, I am the lion."

The king gave permission for everyone to stand up, stormed away and ordered the executioner to take Suleiman's life.

Adaure screamed with fear as the executioner approached where Suleiman, Igwekala and Obinna stood.

Suleiman looked at Obinna who stood next to him and whispered quickly.

"On the day of your execution, ask them to grant your last wish, then find your magic, spare my people but please change this regime and reinstate sanity, peace and love to Tangandoom."

Suleiman spread his arms apart as if he was happy to be slain as the executioner approached with his sword in his right arm. He pushed the sword into Suleiman's stomach and looked in his eyes as life slowly trickled out of him. The executioner pulled the sword out and walked away as

Suleiman's body fell.

Obinna caught his lifeless body and gently placed him on the ground. Some of the maidens wept while others grimaced, and Obinna could see that the king's aides disapproved of the killing.

A warrior handed the executioner a piece of cloth in the palace, which he used to wipe Suleiman's blood off his sword.

Obinna began to breathe slowly. He closed Suleiman's open eyes with his palm and spoke to him.

"Sleep my friend; you can now sleep in peace," he caressed his head, stood up and left Suleiman's lifeless body on the floor.

"What about these three?" the executioner asked the king. "Do you want to keep them alive?" he enquired about Obinna, Igwekala and Adaure.

The king looked over to where Adaure stood. He saw that she was weeping and shaking all over, and he replied.

"Justice is already served; we will execute this one in a month," he referred to Obinna. "Remove him and his friend from the prisons and throw them in the dungeon; keep them there till the day of his execution and give his villagers more work as punishment for what they have done."

The king walked over to Adaure as Suleiman's body was wrapped up in black sheets and spoke calmly to her.

"As for you, I will decide what to do with you later; do not ever disobey Gandoom again," he said. "This will be your final warning."

The king was escorted out from the room by his aides and the executioner accompanied by his warriors pushed Obinna and Igwekala out.

*

They were thrown in the dungeon as the king instructed using ropes attached to a belt which they tied around Obinna and Igwekala's waists and lowered them with ropes into the hole. Those dungeons were the worst place any prisoner in Tangandoom would want to be. They were built by digging holes thirty feet into the ground below the prisons, and the walls were fortified with metal to prevent a prisoner from digging his way out. The only source of light into them was the entrance hole above, and there was not enough airflow.

The king had instructed the warriors to feed Obinna and Igwekala only once a day to punish them. He also requested that they provide minimal amounts of water for them to drink.

Both men had spent three weeks in the dungeon and were dehydrated. They were not allowed to come out and work with the rest of the prisoners while they were in there.

Obinna still had his oja tied around his waist as the warriors did not take it before they threw him in.

Igwekala had become ill again. He was malnourished and found it very difficult to walk properly. His health deteriorated because the dry season, notorious for its low humidity and dust-laden winds had crept in. The temperatures would drop severely in the mornings and at night but would soar in the afternoons. The dust, most of which blots out the sun during the day, made their skin crack, their noses bleed and sometimes made it difficult for them to breathe easily. The dungeon was not suitable to protect them from the harsh weather conditions.

Igwekala had a nervous breakdown in the afternoon, a week before Obinna was due to be executed. His health had improved but he was anxious. He stood next to the walls, repeatedly hitting his head against it and murmuring to himself.

"Igwekala, please try to calm down," Obinna pleaded with him. "Everything will be okay," he reassured.

"No, it will not be okay," Igwekala disagreed. "We have lost it all; there is no hope, you will be dead in a week, and the rest of us will be prisoners here forever."

Igwekala began to punch the wall. He hit it so hard that his wrists began to bleed.

Obinna walked over and held his hands to stop him.

"Igwekala, listen to me," he said. "Please listen."

Igwekala stopped when Obinna held him. Even though he had given up, he was eager to hear what his friend had to say.

"The time has come," Obinna informed him.

"The time for what?" Igwekala asked.

"The time to prepare for war."

Obinna walked away after his response and Igwekala turned around to see where he was going.

Obinna put his hands in the bag, brought out the oja and began to walk back and forth.

"A war between good and evil," he said.

"Obinna, there will be no war," Igwekala objected and shook his head. "Gandoom has a thousand warriors, archers whose arrows will kill you in a second; magicians who will use sorcery to put you in a trance that you will never wake up from," he continued. "What have you got to fight them with?" he asked. "We have got nothing Obinna; nothing."

"I have something," Obinna replied. "The magic of hope and the rhythm of our ancestors."

He walked over to Igwekala and showed him the oja.

"I have the oja, the weapon of my tormented soul and I will sing and play it for the enemy; they will have no choice but to listen to it."

Obinna pulled Igwekala's arm and spoke to him sternly. There was a fire in his eyes as he spoke. He looked upset and fed up, which made Igwekala even more worried.

"So, come Igwekala, let us dance and prepare for war; I have fought the enemy inside of me, the doubt and hopelessness; if they put me to death in a week, you will be the one to lead Umuzura's dance; you will finish my song and tell them that all is well; yes all is well."

And he led Igwekala by the arm as both men began to dance while he played the oja. They both danced around each other in circles and Igwekala would occasionally call out to Obinna as the melody from the oja became more intense.

Even though he was limping and in pain, he refused to stop.

"We have nothing to lose so we might as well dance," Igwekala said.

Both men danced till sunset. They jumped up and down in their dungeon while Obinna's oja serenaded the air with its melody.

They did not care about who was listening to them or about the next day. They danced and danced until they were both tired.

Igwekala had calmed down and was not nervous anymore. He still limped, but the pain in his leg suddenly felt better.

They both hugged each other and laughed through the night until they fell asleep.

*

The day for Obinna's execution had finally arrived. The king wanted him to be publicly executed during Tangandoom's dry season festival in the arena.

Those sorts of executions took place occasionally, and the crowd liked it; they saw it as part of their entertainment.

They had already decorated the arena for the festival. Beautiful flowers and trees were planted all around the edges of walls and temporary stalls built for food, drinks and water.

There was a structure built with stone and covered with leaves where they slaughtered animals to offer sacrifices to the gods and appease them to ensure that the rain comes back after the dry season had passed.

The warriors decorated the floor on which the king would walk. They covered it with leopard's skin from the passageways to the central podium, which was raised a few feet above the ground and had steps built for the king to walk to the top.

Each passageway had lions tied to ropes that they nailed into the ground, and a warrior stood nearby with a spear and shield in hand.

There were drummers, dancers and performers who had all been practising their various acts of entertainment before the festival began. The maidens from the king's palace had also decorated themselves with beads which they wore around their necks and waists.

All Gandoom's warriors had their bodies painted and

decorated with black tribal marks as they would also perform their war dances for the king. The executioner was the most decorated. He walked around bare-chested, with the tattoo of the rising sun on his chest in full display. He also had eagle feathers tied to his arms and wore a heavy bead around his neck which had pendants made from the teeth of a lion.

The king's magicians had taken their positions as well. They stood in one corner, burnt firewood and incense as they chanted incantations from books that they had with them.

All spectators for the festival had started to sit down in the several rows of seats built around the arena in circles surrounding the central podium.

The prisoners from Obinna's village were also there but were all made to sit on the floor where they could see all the activities as they went on.

Twelve armed warriors operated the main entrance gate; they divided themselves into two groups. Each group of six warriors stood on one side facing the other group.

Two young boys also stood right next to the gates holding long whips.

The festival officially started around midday. The executioner had sharpened his sword against a stone to prepare for Obinna's execution.

The king's magicians were the first to walk through the arena. They had a buffalo on a leash which they led to the structure covered with leaves to offer sacrifices. They tied the buffalo to a stick and waited for the festival to begin.

The executioner appeared, accompanied by a few warriors who walked alongside him. He was welcomed with cheers and claps as the arena erupted when they saw him.

The executioner drew his sword and charged his warriors

who all ran away with their heads lowered. It was his display of authority which everyone understood as they continued cheering and clapping.

"Rulership is the natural order of things," the executioner bellowed, and the crowd became silent. "The lion rules the jungle and the sea monster rules the ocean, day rules over the night," he continued, "Tangandoom, behold the rising sun is here, our king and ruler Gandoom is here."

The crowd, including the executioner, immediately knelt and lowered their heads as the king emerged with his entourage through a passageway.

As the king walked on the leopard's skin laid down for him, maidens and young women began to roll on the floor as he walked past, and some were singing songs of praise to him.

Adaure was not amongst the maidens. She had been allowed to be with the king's entourage, who followed him into the arena.

The king had requested that she should no longer partake in any form of work as she was due to give birth to her baby anytime soon.

"Rising Sun, we are alive because you have made it possible," the maidens sang as he walked along.

The king had a smile on his face. He had been decorated with expensive clothing made from the skin of a cheetah and wore gold beads and necklaces for the festival. He majestically walked to the podium at the centre, stood at the top and informed the crowd that they could look at him.

"Tangandoom, is it not fair to say that what we have achieved is apparent and will echo through eternity?" the king asked as he calmly looked at everyone gathered.

The crowd nodded their heads to show the king that they agreed with what he said.

"All of you have contributed to this greatness and made our lands fertile; you have worked hard all through the rains and now that the dry season is upon us, let us rejoice at this festival and offer sacrifices to the gods so they can see us through the dryness, so that we may continue to live in abundance."

The crowd erupted with cheers again as Gandoom concluded his speech and indicated that the festival had officially started.

He walked down from the podium and requested one of his aides to bring Udele, the parrot as he walked to the throne built for him in the arena.

The parrot was brought out in her cage, released and gently placed on a perch next to the king's throne as he sat down.

The executioner came out again to meet loud cheers from the crowd. He summoned the magicians to proceed with their sacrifice before other activities commenced.

The magicians who were all dressed in long black robes walked over to the buffalo, one of them brought out a long blade and killed the animal. The buffalo's blood trickled into a cup which one of the magicians held, he raised the cup above his head and moved his hands three times in a circular motion before speaking.

"Let this buffalo blood that we have shed exonerate us from calamity," he said as he poured a few drops of the blood on the ground.

"Let the gods accept this sacrifice, empower and shine their light upon us through their chosen vessel; their chosen vessel who is Gandoom, the rising sun." they revered the king.

The magicians took a sip of the blood and passed the cup to the others who also drank from it.

The magicians queued up and made way for the warriors who came out to perform their war dance for the king.

The executioner led the warriors into the arena as they danced, thumped their chests, and stamped their feet on the ground. He drew his sword and asked a warrior at the passageway entrance to release one of the lions.

Everyone in the open part of the arena left when they heard his request. They understood that it was a tradition for the executioner to fight a lion during the festival, and they all went to safe areas where the lion could not reach them to observe what was happening.

The warrior released the lion and ran to the safe areas while Gandoom watched keenly with a smile on his face.

The executioner charged the lion as it approached him, grabbed it by its mane and wrestled it to the ground. He held the animal there to show the crowd that he had power over the beast, rereleased it and retreated. He had sustained a deep cut on his right arm from the lion's claws which had started to bleed, but he did not show signs of pain from the injury.

The king applauded him from where he sat and nodded to show that he was pleased with the performance.

The executioner drew his weapon when the lion charged him again and killed it with one swipe of his sword.

The crowd erupted, cheering and clapping for him as he ran around the arena with his arms held up in victory.

He was approached by another warrior who used a piece of cloth to wrap the wound he sustained.

"Tangandoom marvels at your strength," the warrior said to him as he helped clean his wounds.

"This is nothing," the executioner boasted, "I crush men and beasts with my bare hands."

It was a tradition in Tangandoom that any prisoner who is about to be executed is fed his last meal and granted a last wish, so the executioner informed the warrior to go to Obinna's dungeon and ask him what he wanted to eat.

The warrior went as the executioner instructed.

He saw Obinna and Igwekala sitting on the floor in silence when he looked down at them from the entrance.

"They have requested me to ask you what you want to eat," he informed Obinna. "This would be your last meal on this earth, and if I were you, I would ask for something outstanding," he teased.

Obinna looked up at him and replied with a raised voice:

"I would like some cocoyam for my friend, some charcoal and a cup of palm oil for me."

"Cocoyam, charcoal and palm oil?" the warrior laughed, "You could not have thought of anything better?" He shook his head and agreed, "So be it."

When the warrior left, Obinna turned to Igwekala and asked,

"Are you okay?"

Igwekala did not respond, and Obinna touched him on the shoulder.

"What is the matter, Igwekala?" he asked. "You look worried."

Igwekala burst into tears; he covered his face with his palms as he wept uncontrollably.

"This was not how I thought it would end for you; you

were such a nice young man," he cried. "I will avenge your death Obinna; they will not get away with this."

Obinna rubbed Igwekala's shoulder to console him and replied.

"Vengeance is for the gods; let them decide when to hand it to our enemies."

Igwekala sniffed and cleared his throat so he could speak clearly and asked Obinna a question.

"They say that when we die, some of us join our ancestors as stars in the sky, right?"

"Yes," Obinna replied. "Our transformed bodies and pure souls illuminate the skies, and our ears will be open, listening to the wishes and songs of our loved ones at night when they sing and dance in the moonlight."

Igwekala agreed and nodded.

"When you pass away today, I want you to be the North star; the brightest one that sits still at night so I can talk to you for hours before I sleep," he told Obinna.

The warrior who went to bring their meal returned as they spoke and threw the food and a bottle of palm oil with the charcoal, wrapped in leaves through the hole above their dungeon and left.

Obinna offered Igwekala the cocoyam, but he declined.

"I have lost my appetite," he said. "What is the charcoal for?" he asked Obinna.

"It is our symbol of war; we are warriors now," Obinna replied. "Stand up, Igwekala." Igwekala stood up with Obinna, and he began to dissolve the charcoal in the palm oil as he spoke, stirred the mixture properly with his fingers and walked over to him.

"You are now an ordained warrior, like the Idanuwo

warriors we have at Umuzura and you will fight alongside me," he told him as he drew two lines on Igwekala's forehead and two on each side of his cheek with the charcoal. He also marked his forehead and cheeks with the charcoal.

"Obinna, my heart is broken, and I am tired; I feel your pain, but I will stand by you and fight your war," Igwekala promised him. "They will kill us both out there, but I will not go down without a fight," he continued, "you see, I do not have much to live for; I am not wealthy, neither do I have a wife nor children," he lamented. "All I have is my word, and I say to you that I am willing to die with you today."

Obinna smiled at Igwekala and held his shoulders with both hands.

"But if we are warriors, what would our names be?" he asked Obinna. "Remember, all the warriors in our village have names which are not the ones given to them at birth; I want a name that will sound great in our village's history books after we die."

Obinna gave it a thought and replied:

"You will be known as the limping king."

He waited to see if Igwekala liked the name he had proposed for him.

"Limping king?" Igwekala asked and smiled, "I do surely limp, but king?" he asked, "I think that is a bit farfetched." He smiled again and continued, "I like it, so limping king it is then," he agreed.

"What about you?" Igwekala asked. "What would yours be?"

Both men heard a warrior open their dungeon from above, and they both looked up. The warrior let the rope and belt down the hole and spoke to them.

"Your time is up, put that around your waist now; Tangandoom is waiting to see your blood spill."

Obinna made sure his oja was appropriately tied around his waist, grabbed the rope first with enthusiasm, looked at Igwekala who had started panicking already and replied.

"Mine will be oja; the magician."

He secured the belt around his waist, and as they pulled him up slowly, Igwekala looked up at him.

As he was being pulled up, he felt his entire life flash quickly before his eyes, his strengths, and weaknesses. He had regrets and thought about things he would have done differently; he felt a bit of hatred towards Tangandoom but quickly suppressed it.

Thoughts about love, hate and human nature, went through his mind.

He understood love; he found it first in Adaure's eyes.

She was pregnant, but what mattered was how he could protect her and Umuzura from hate.

But he had no doubts; that day he could feel a fire burning within him, that spread through his chest, down to his fingers and toes.

Even though he had not fully understood it, he knew what he felt; it was the fire of magic.

Obinna got to the top and was pulled out by a warrior who removed the belt in his waist and put chains on his hands and feet.

The warrior let the rope down again and pulled Igwekala up.

The warrior led them on as lambs led to the slaughter, holding the long end of the chain.

The passageway they went through was silent, and all

Obinna heard were the chains around their hands and feet clattering as they staggered along.

The performances at the arena had stopped. Someone announced to the crowd that it was time to carry out a prisoner execution, and they eagerly waited for it.

As they emerged through the passageway into the arena, the bright sunshine made Obinna squint as it had been a while since he came outside.

Igwekala was separated and taken to where the rest of his villagers sat while they led Obinna to the central podium.

When he got on top, he quickly looked around and spotted Adaure standing with the king's aides near his throne.

Adaure smiled at him with tears flowing down her cheeks, and she felt her baby kick in her womb. She rubbed her belly and spoke to her unborn child.

"Look, there is your father, and he will always love you," she said.

The king looked at Adaure and noticed she was crying. It became clear to him that she and Obinna were emotionally connected. The executioner's allegations were right, and the execution was fully justified, the king thought.

Obinna looked across to the king and saw Udele, the parrot on her perch. The parrot flapped and spread its wings as soon as she saw Obinna and began to say "Prophecy, prophecy," repetitively.

Obinna felt unwell as usual whenever that happened. He felt dizzy, and his hands and feet became cold. He staggered a bit but forced himself to overcome that feeling and managed to stay upright on his feet.

He could feel his heartbeat as the executioner emerged with his sword in the scabbard he carried. He raised the sword to the crowd, and they all clapped and cheered in anticipation as he walked over to Obinna and forced him on his knees.

The executioner greeted Gandoom with a bow and addressed the crowd.

"Tangandoom, behold; a traitor, a liar and our king's enemy," he accused. "He will be slain to honour the rule of the land and following the instruction of the Rising Sun; our king, Gandoom."

The sky that day was clear, and the dry, harsh winds blew gently on Obinna's neck as he knelt. His head felt heavy on his shoulders as if he was carrying a burden, and he could see the sweat from his forehead drip onto the ground from the heat of the sun.

He took deep breaths with his eyes closed and thought of Suleiman. He remembered what Suleiman said to him the day he was slain and also the writing on his prison wall.

He thought about Suleiman's words exactly as he said it:

"On the day of your execution, ask them to grant your last wish, then find your magic, spare my people but please change this regime and reinstate sanity, peace and love to Tangandoom."

He repeated the words of the writing on the wall.

"To find your way out, you must first find your way in, for the keys that you seek are with and within you."

The time to think was over, and Obinna felt it was time to act.

The executioner had walked up the podium and drawn his sword from its scabbard, waiting for the king to give the order to execute Obinna.

The king stood up, and the crowd became silent, eagerly

waiting for him to give the order.

Adaure took a deep breath, closed her eyes and said:

"Human, I enjoyed my time with you; it was worth it."

Igwekala looked away too. He could not bear the sight.

As the king raised his right arm to speak, Obinna interrupted him. His voice bellowed through the arena.

"Gandoom!" he called out to the king, "I demand that you grant my last wish; it is a tradition and your law so you must honour it."

The executioner looked at the king and raised his sword above his head. He wanted to proceed with the execution quickly.

"Wait," the king told the executioner. "We will honour the rule of the land; allow the one who is about to die to make his last wish."

The king knew that even though it was a prisoner's right to make the last wish on the day of their execution, he did not necessarily have to fulfil the request as it all depended on what the prisoner demands.

Adaure opened her eyes when she heard what Obinna said, and the crowd was eager to listen to what he was going to demand.

A voice yelled out from where Obinna's villagers sat.

"Obinna, ask the king to set us free! Tell these evil men to let us go."

The man who spoke was Ekwueme, that elder in Umuzura who was always drunk. He was fearless and did not care about what might happen to him for disrespecting the king. Some of the villagers who sat near him covered his mouth with their palms to prevent him from speaking again as they feared for his life.

Obinna did not make that request. He asked for something different and somewhat bizarre.

"I request to perform for you and the crowd with my oja. It speaks, and it wants to talk to all of you."

The executioner waited for the king's response. His patience was beginning to run out.

The king thought about it. He looked around at everyone present and felt that he had to honour his own rules. He understood that it would look bad if he declined and allowed the execution to proceed without accepting Obinna's request. After all, it was a simple request, the king thought, and perhaps, it would keep the crowd entertained.

"The Rising Sun is always fair and just; your wish is granted." The king accepted and sat down.

The executioner lowered his sword. He was not pleased with the king's decision.

He placed the sword back in its sheath and spoke to Obinna.

"You see, I told you before; wherever you go, a sword will always defeat a flute," he reminded Obinna about the conversation they had on their way to Tangandoom.

"These are the ones you want to perform for?" he asked, referring to the crowd. "They are not interested in your flute; they are here to watch you die, drink your blood and then feast on your flesh."

Obinna got up, took three steps backwards, slowly brought out the flute from the bag around his waist and replied:

"They will not see me die today; they are my audience, and this is my stage."

What happened afterwards was worthy of being written

in stone and placed at the entrance to the gates of eternity and on the bosom of mothers during childbirth, so that those who are born would spread its message, and those who die would take it with them while they pass away.

He spoke to them that day with the oja and taught them about hope, faith and magic.

Three steps to the left; three to the right, up and down, he jumped like a warrior till the universe heard his melody.

Obinna found his magic and harnessed its powers using the oja.

As he blew into it, he called upon the wind, and it answered.

A strong gust blew through the arena. It blew thick clouds across the skies as the sun became blotted out, and the day became night. The winds turned into a gale that toppled everything it came across.

The chains around Obinna's hands and legs snapped to pieces.

Stalls, stands and animals were lifted into the air, people in the arena were pushed to the ground by its force as they tried to make sense of what was happening.

Lightning struck, and thunder followed as Obinna leapt into the air, dancing with his arms spread out.

The executioner and all his warriors staggered and fell over. The look on his face seemed as though he had seen a ghost.

Surely, Obinna did look like a spirit being that day. The black part of his eyeballs went away, and his pure white eyes glared at everything he looked at as though he was possessed.

The power of the oja and its magic possessed him.

Gandoom held unto his throne helplessly as the winds

shook him.

All the beads and decorations he wore blew away, and he looked terrified and helpless.

Udele, the parrot flew up in the skies screaming, "Prophecy, prophecy!" but did not do so for long as the winds blew the parrot across the arena and struck her against a wall. The parrot fell on the floor and could not get up.

Igwekala fell over too but looked up at Obinna with a smile from where he lay and called out to him.

"Oja, the magician," he called out to him twice, "great warrior of Umuzura, you will live; you will live."

Obinna spun around as he performed and called upon water, and it responded.

Thunderstorms followed as heavy rain pelted everyone. Rain drenched Obinna from head to toe.

The executioner and Gandoom got up, tried to run and take shelter, but Obinna did not let them go. He kept them entertained and tortured them.

Obinna beat his chest twice and squared up to the executioner with his arms spread but holding the oja.

The executioner reached for his sword but had no energy left in him to draw it. He fell again looking helplessly at Obinna as he cowered over him.

Obinna took three steps back, snarled, gnashed his teeth and summoned earth as he jumped high up.

Earth came to his rescue when he descended. The ground under their feet shook vigorously as statues and structures gave in and fell to pieces.

The part of the podium on which the executioner stood broke off, and he was thrown to the ground, wriggling with pain.

Seats in the arena fell to pieces, and people tried their best to hold onto anything near them for their dear lives.

Obinna fell on his knees with his eyes closed and remembered Adaure.

She sat on the floor, clutching her belly and observing all that was happening with a big smile on her face.

He gasped for breath but blew a gentle song into the oja. He was worried and thought that perhaps his magic had shaken her and the baby too much.

His music pleaded with earth for calmness and requested fire not to get involved.

And they both obeyed. The ground gradually became quiet, and silence took over. The thick clouds went away, and the sky became bright again.

What they heard afterwards was a loud cry; it was a baby.

Adaure's water had broken instantly, and she had given birth there at the arena. The trauma had shaken her, and the baby was born prematurely, a few weeks earlier than expected, and it was a girl.

She had cut the umbilical cord herself and lay with the baby, taking very deep breaths and could not move from the fatigue.

Igwekala saw that she had given birth and most people in the arena heard the baby crying but could not do anything to help.

Everyone in the arena was shaken and gradually tried to pick themselves from the ground.

The executioner staggered up from where he lay but was still dazed. He found pieces of his sword on the ground, and its casing also was torn to bits.

The warriors at the gates also looked confused and worn out.

Obinna looked around at everyone and heaved a sigh of relief. He did not notice that Adaure had given birth.

He raised his voice and called out as he slowly stepped down from the podium:

"He whom destiny has chosen, come with me now; we are free."

He looked straight ahead, kept walking and did not look back.

The executioner and some of his warriors tried to stop him but could not. Their feet felt as if an unseen force chained them to the ground, and they could not move at all.

Earth held them as hostages.

Obinna's villagers tried to follow him but could not. Their feet were held to the ground too by the unknown force.

Obinna was heading towards the entrance gates. Each majestic step he took, shook the ground.

He had walked past all the warriors through the centre of the arena unharmed and turned around as he approached the gates to see who was following him.

He saw Igwekala limping towards him, and he smiled and waited.

When Igwekala got reasonably close, he turned towards the gates and continued walking.

"Open those gates, stand aside now and let us pass," he commanded the dazed warriors at the gates.

The warriors obeyed, grabbed the gates and flung it open without saying a word. They seemed confused and looked like they were all put into a trance.

The king was in shock as he sat on the floor with his

mouth open, watching what was happening.

Igwekala limped faster and called out to Obinna.

"Obinna, stop!" he yelled., "Adaure has just given birth; I saw it, I saw it," he cried.

As soon as Obinna heard what Igwekala told him, he turned around and tried to run in the direction where Adaure lay but an unknown force pushed him back, and he staggered and almost lost balance. He refused to give up and tried again to overcome the energy that prevented him from moving. He exerted more effort and cried out:

"No, please let me go; I cannot leave her here with my baby."

But the earth refused.

Obinna threw the oja on the floor with frustration and tried with all his might to run towards her. He wanted to let go of the omen and save Adaure and his baby. They were more important to him at that moment.

When the oja hit the floor, the earth shook so vigorously that it pushed Obinna backwards, away from his intended direction and toppled him over.

Igwekala fell too, and more structures gave in and crashed to the ground blowing a considerable amount of dust and debris into the air.

Obinna lay there, helpless and gasping for breath.

Earth had tortured him with love, but he did not understand why that was his purpose or his destiny.

Obinna realised that it was not his destiny to take Adaure and the baby with him then. He slowly got up when the dust settled, picked the oja from the ground, looked across to where Adaure was and saw her lying with the baby whose body was wet and covered with dust and sand.

The baby was alive as he could see she was moving.

He knew he had no choice but to continue his journey without them.

He felt it, so he turned around and continued walking towards the entrance gates without looking back again.

"Wait, there is someone else following us," Igwekala gasped as he too picked himself up.

Obinna turned around and saw who it was. It was Ekwueme, the drunk elder.

His feet were also released, and he ran across the arena towards Obinna, holding part of his garment so it would not fall off.

"Obinna, wait; we have to go back and get the rest of our villagers," Igwekala demanded.

"No," Obinna refused. "It is not yet their destiny. Those who are destined to follow me are already here."

Igwekala looked around as they walked and tried to change Obinna's mind.

"But only Ekwueme is following us," he lamented. "Are you sure about this?" he asked.

"Ekwueme is just an old drunkard, and I am not sure he is ready for this journey," he whispered to Obinna as Ekwueme got close.

Ekwueme caught up with them, and Igwekala noticed he was holding a small keg filled with wine as he approached. Ekwueme had seen the item on the floor, amongst the ruins and picked it up before he ran to them. He knew fully well that it was wine, and he would not miss an opportunity to have a drink.

Igwekala became even more sceptical when he saw what he held.

"Obinna, seriously, this man will not survive this journey; look, he even took a keg of wine with him."

Ekwueme joined them and interrupted when he looked at Obinna's eyeballs which were still white.

"Your eyes look very scary," he said. "It seems spirits have possessed you."

Obinna hesitantly smiled at him as his eyeballs gradually changed back to normal and said:

"Warriors chosen by destiny, follow me; we are on our way home."

The three men walked behind Obinna as he led them on, straight through the twelve warriors at the gates they passed without looking back.

Obinna felt very sad that Adaure was unable to follow him, but he was not afraid. He knew that was the way it was meant to be. He believed that he would return when the time was right to get her, his baby and the rest. Destiny had chosen his comrades; two inexperienced warriors that would fight his battle alongside him; an old drunkard and a man that limps.

The three men walked through the gates, and the warriors from Tangandoom shut it behind them.

Obinna stopped, looked around and took a deep breath. He felt elated as he looked further ahead at the fields in front of them. They had never gone that far on their own.

Ekwueme gulped down some of the wine he had while Igwekala looked at him with disgust. The drunkard was happier than the rest as he ran around them with excitement.

"We are free!" he shrieked. "I cannot believe this."

"Obinna, where do we go from here?" Igwekala asked. "What should we do?"

Obinna put the oja back in the bag tied around his waist and replied:

"We must hurry and go towards the east; we will find help when we get there."

The nearest village in the east was Kanuri; its inhabitants were animal farmers, and their king was known as Nuri. Kanuri had a cordial relationship with Obinna's community, but neither he nor Igwekala had been there before.

The drunkard being the eldest of the three, had visited the village when he was young and had vague memories about them. His father took him there on a few occasions to trade as the village was known for its success in breeding farm animals. But the drunkard also remembered something his father told him, peculiar about the community; they lived as if there was no tomorrow. They believed that humans were born to enjoy and celebrate life to the fullest and must do everything necessary to be happy because, after death, there would be nothing else to expect.

Igwekala spoke as they walked and advised Obinna.

"The nearest village to the east is Kanuri, a land of goats, sheep and cattle. They do not have anything more to offer us to fight Gandoom with."

"It is a magnificent village," the drunkard interrupted, "they have rivers flowing with wine and the most beautiful women your eyes have ever seen."

Obinna interrupted him, raised his right hand to get them to pay attention and calmly spoke.

"The curse still follows us; look at the skies."

The two men looked up and saw Udele, the parrot hovering above them. She had regained consciousness and flown over the gates.

The drunkard became very upset when he saw the bird and picked up stones from the ground to throw and scare the parrot away.

Obinna held his hands and stopped him.

"There's no need for that," he said. "This is how it was meant to be; the curse will be broken at the appointed time."

"But Udele is our curse," the drunkard insisted. "As long as this parrot is alive, we will continue to suffer, so I suggest we find a way to lure and capture this evil bird and kill it."

"Do not bear anger in your heart," Obinna told him. "Udele is only a bird fulfilling her purpose, and when that purpose is complete, Udele will go away," he explained.

"Come, we do not have much time; run, follow me towards the east." Obinna said.

Obinna looked up but could not see the bird as she had flown away, he looked behind to ensure that the warriors from Tangandoom were not following them and ran towards the east with the drunkard and Igwekala running behind him.

Chapter Four

The distance from Tangandoom to Kanuri was about three hundred miles. They would have to walk through a vast expanse of barren land which led to a hill, then walk through a thick forest that had footpaths that led to a river. The three men had walked the entire afternoon and needed to get some rest.

The drunkard had become drunk from the wine he had with him and could not walk straight. He had almost finished the wine in the keg all by himself.

Igwekala had to hold him sometimes so he would not fall over.

Obinna decided that they had to find shelter somewhere.

"It is getting dark now, and we have to find somewhere to sleep; Ekwueme needs to rest," Obinna said.

"No, I am fine." Ekwueme slurred, "I feel like I can reach out and touch the moon; I feel great."

"You are not okay," Igwekala interrupted, "you are drunk and need to sleep it off."

"Let us make a fire over there to keep us warm, and we can sleep under that mango tree," Obinna informed them.

The drunkard began to laugh at Obinna's suggestion. He thought that it was a ridiculous request and did not hesitate to tell Obinna how he felt.

"Obinna, it has rained, and the ground is wet; you cannot make fire with sticks that are wet," he argued.

Obinna smiled at him but insisted that they should pick up the wet sticks as firewood. He helped them as Igwekala, and the drunkard gathered the sticks and laid them in a pile near the mango tree.

"We have firewood now but nothing to start the fire with," the drunkard reminded them.

Obinna began to walk around the firewood in circles. He told his friends to sit down and stay still as he carried on. He brought out the oja from the bag around his waist and responded to the drunkard.

"When you have the power of magic, you will understand that everything is possible."

He played a short song with the oja and called upon the element, fire.

"I pleaded with you earlier to stay away to protect Adaure; the love of my life, but I ask you now to manifest; light these wet sticks so three warriors can stay warm tonight," Obinna requested.

Igwekala and the drunkard were shocked as the wet sticks ignited. The firewood burned as if they poured oils over them as fuel.

Igwekala began to clap and scream with excitement.

"Oja, oja, the magician," he praised Obinna. "My eyes have seen unimaginable things today, and I thank our ancestors for these powers they have given you."

The three men sat around the fire and warmed themselves up.

Igwekala felt the time was right to ask Obinna questions about all that had happened. He and Ekwueme began to interrogate him about things they did not understand.

"How are you able to do these things that I have witnessed?" Igwekala asked Obinna.

He reached out and asked Obinna to give him the oja, and he did.

Igwekala looked carefully at it, raised and looked through its holes. He blew into the oja but let out a loud noise as he did not know how to use the flute.

"But it is only a flute, so how come it can do these things?" Igwekala asked. "I saw what happened back there; how the earth shook and how you cast a spell on those warriors."

Igwekala stood up with the oja; he wanted more answers to his questions. He looked up at the mango tree, which they sat underneath and spoke.

"The oja is magical isn't it?" he asked. "So by the power that lies within this flute, I ask that fruits should fall from the branches of this tree now so that we may eat," he commanded, eager to see what would happen.

The drunkard paid keen attention to what Igwekala was doing even though he was drunk.

Nothing happened when Igwekala made the request.

He blew into the oja again and repeated his request, but the fruits did not fall from the tree, so he sat down, frustrated and asked Obinna a question.

"Obinna, nothing happened," he complained. "So is it the oja that can do these things or is it you?" he asked.

The drunkard laughed when he saw Igwekala trying to make fruits fall from the tree.

"Igwekala, give it up; you cannot even make reasonable music with the oja, let alone conjure magic with it," the drunkard joked.

Igwekala kissed his teeth at him and asked Obinna again:

"Please tell me, is it you or the oja that is responsible for all these magical things happening?"

"It is both of us," Obinna replied. "I am now one with the oja; it feels what I feel, and it creates magic because I feel it very strongly."

"I do not understand," Igwekala said. "It creates magic because you feel it strongly?" he asked, "But I felt strongly about getting fruits from this mango tree, and it did not happen."

"It did not happen because you did not feel it strongly enough; you did not want it well enough," Obinna responded and took the oja from Igwekala.

He got up, brushed the grass and sand off his clothes with his left hand and began to walk around his friends while the fire burned.

"Everyone has an oja; most people do not even realise that they do because doubt, fear and distractions consume them."

He stopped in front of the drunkard as if he was talking directly to him and continued.

"Anything can be your oja; like those keys you held to the masquerade huts at Umuzura, or these stones on the ground, even your wine keg, Ekwueme."

"You speak with so much confidence and knowledge now," Igwekala told Obinna. "How are you so sure about the things that you are saying?" he asked. "How do you know these things?"

"I know because I am now alive," Obinna replied. "I can now hear the words in the songs of trees when they sway, I understand the language that thunder and lightning speak, and I can see even when I close my eyes; I can feel it all through magic, and it feels wonderful."

He got Ekwueme's full attention that moment he spoke about wine. He was very eager to understand what Obinna was explaining.

"Most people spend their lives looking for that special thing that will create magic and change everything else; little do they know that they had it all the while they were searching," Obinna added.

"Hmm," the drunkard rubbed his chin as he thought about what Obinna said.

"Obinna, it is hard to believe what you are saying," he slurred. "If we all have the power of magic then why are you the only one that can conjure it?" he asked. "Why are you the only one it works for?"

Obinna asked him to stand up, and he did with a bit of effort. He gave him the oja and asked him to pick up his wine keg from the ground.

"I want you to close your eyes and think of something now that you want badly; something that you can give everything for so that you can have it."

The drunkard did as Obinna instructed. He took a sip from the keg, thought about wine and wished he had a lot more to drink. He imagined that he was swimming in a river made from wine and imagined himself being drunk and happy. He believed that the river made of wine was his and it was flowing for him to enjoy forever.

"What did you think of?" Obinna asked him.

"I thought of palm wine; the finest quality tapped in the morning, and I imagined myself swimming in a river made from it," the drunkard managed to speak with several hiccups.

"Ridiculous," Igwekala interrupted.

Obinna asked him to hold that thought firmly in his mind and blow into the oja. He also told him to take another sip of his wine, stand before the tree and ask for the fruits to fall as Igwekala tried earlier without success.

"You might have your wish come true if you believe," Obinna told him.

The drunkard did so and spoke to the mango tree.

Igwekala was shocked when he felt a strong wind shake the branches of the tree. Mango fruits began to fall from the branches as the drunkard ran further way to avoid getting hit by the fruits.

Obinna smiled when he saw how excited the drunkard was about what happened.

The drunkard began to jump up and down, clapping and praising himself with joy as he ran back to the tree.

"I did it; I did it," he repeated and looked at Obinna with surprise.

"Yes, you did." Obinna nodded, took the oja from him and put it back in his bag.

"So, does that mean that I will get my river of wine then?" he asked and placed the wine keg on the ground. "That was my wish."

Obinna smiled and replied:

"I do not know; the oja might not give you what will kill you; it controls the elements of nature: earth, wind, water and fire," he explained. "It controls the elements to work for the common good, in favour of the bearer who conjures magic with it."

The drunkard was not very pleased with his explanation. He frowned, bent over and picked some fruits from the ground and began to eat. He offered some to Igwekala and Obinna too, and they accepted. The three men sat by the fire and ate to their fill as the night passed.

"Are you worried about Adaure and your newborn baby?" Igwekala asked.

"Yes, I am," Obinna replied.

"What?" the drunkard asked. "What baby are you talking about?"

"Obinna's child," said Igwekala. "Adaure gave birth at the arena before we escaped."

"Ha!" he screamed with excitement, tried to jump up but staggered as he was not sober yet. "Wonderful. You see, I told you both that I feel great about today, it is a beautiful day."

The drunkard began to dance with mangoes in one hand while holding his garment at the waist with the other, which made Obinna and Igwekala laugh.

"Is the baby okay?" he asked as he stopped dancing. His head had begun to spin, and he felt dizzy.

"Yes, the baby is alive," Igwekala replied and helped him to sit down on the ground.

"I wonder if it is a boy or a girl?" Igwekala asked.

"I do not know," Obinna replied.

"The baby is a girl," the drunkard interrupted.

Obinna and Igwekala paused, looked at each other with surprise and asked him how he knew that, simultaneously.

"How do you know the baby is a girl?" Obinna asked him again.

"Oh, I thought you were the magician," the drunkard

joked. "How is it possible that you do not know?"

"Unfortunately, I do not," Obinna admitted.

The drunkard laughed again and replied;

"Young men, you have a lot to learn," he explained. "The baby is a girl because I feel it strongly; yes, I feel it," he slurred.

"Why do I feel it?" he asked them. "Because of this," he continued and picked the wine keg up to show Obinna and Igwekala.

Igwekala interrupted him and asked:

"Ekwueme, you know the baby is a girl because you have had some wine to drink?"

"Yes, of course," he replied. "I found this wine on the ground where Adaure gave birth; I drank it and now, look at me; I am happy." The drunkard spread his arms apart to emphasise how he felt.

"It is all a sign," he revealed to them. "The baby, the wine and my happiness; yes, it is all connected," he insisted. "You see, young men, nothing makes a man happier than wine and a woman so, that baby is a girl."

Obinna looked at Igwekala to see his reaction, and they both burst into laughter.

Igwekala laughed so hard that tears trickled from the corner of his eyes. He found the drunkard's explanation ridiculous.

The drunkard looked at them with wide eyes as though he did not understand the reason for their laughter.

"You have to stop drinking, Ekwueme," Igwekala advised him. "Too much wine will be the cause of your death someday if you do not stop."

The drunkard became upset. He went over to Igwekala,

held the keg up for him to see and replied,

"You see this wine?" he showed him. "The gods put it here for me to enjoy; it is my best friend."

"Or your worst enemy," Igwekala added.

"No, this enemy is one which I know very well; the enemy you know is better than the friend you do not know," he replied. "Obinna's baby is a girl because I feel it; I am telling you what I feel; period."

"You do not know what you are saying," Igwekala interrupted again.

Obinna had to intervene to calm things down and said to the drunkard:

"Then hold onto your feelings, Ekwueme; sometimes, it is better to feel than to know."

The drunkard gulped down some more wine. He was pleased with Obinna's response and sat down with them smiling.

"Life is short and meaningless," he said. "Let us drink and celebrate Obinna's good news," he maintained. "We will all die eventually, anyway."

He smiled at Igwekala to show him that he was not bothered by their argument, left the wine near Obinna and stretched himself out on the ground.

The drunkard was the first to fall asleep and began to snore loudly while Obinna and Igwekala lay side by side as the firewood burned. Igwekala was full of thought and found it hard to sleep. His belly would occasionally rumble from all the mango he ate, and he would adjust himself where he lay to stop the stomach rumbling. Both men lay on their backs, staring at the full moon in the sky. Igwekala felt bad that he was unable to make the fruits fall from the tree, he felt a bit disappointed and wondered why and how the drunkard was able to do so and he could not.

Igwekala began to speak but was abruptly interrupted by Obinna.

"Shh, listen." Obinna held Igwekala by the arm to stop him from speaking. "Do you hear it?" he asked Igwekala.

"Hear what?" Igwekala asked. "The rustling noise in the grass nearby? he queried., "Or is it the birds singing in the tree above our heads?"

He told Obinna that the noise in the grass could be an animal making its way home for the night.

"Do you want me to go and check the bushes to see what it was?" he asked Obinna.

"No," Obinna objected. "I do not mean those."

"I meant the silence," Obinna clarified, paused and began to speak again:

"The silence has a voice; it is talking to itself and us; I can hear all that it is saying."

Igwekala listened but did not understand what Obinna was telling him.

The bird in the tree stopped singing, and the rustling noise in the bushes stopped when Igwekala paid attention.

"Yes, I understand that it is quiet, but I cannot hear anything," Igwekala objected. "How can silence have a voice?" he asked Obinna, "What is it saying?"

Obinna did not look at Igwekala at all. He continued staring at the full moon as he spoke.

"It is having a conversation and asking questions about love, hate, greed; about good and evil."

The drunkard snored when Obinna spoke which made Igwekala jump a bit.

"Obinna are you hearing ghosts speaking?" Igwekala asked. "You are scaring me a little bit."

"The silence is asking questions about we humans," Obinna continued with a very distant look in his eyes and began to look around as though he was confused. "It is worried about us and does not understand some of the things we do and why we do it."

Igwekala got up from where he lay and sat closer to Obinna. He was scared and replied.

"This silence that you speak of, can it not help us, humans, then?" he asked. "Can it not change us into something that it can understand or change us for the better?"

"It says that it always helps us, but change is our choice to make," Obinna replied. "The silence is talking to this tree above us now."

"What is it telling the tree?" Igwekala asked.

"It is telling the tree to live; that it will plead with the rain to return soon and help her to produce more fruit and replace the ones that fell for us so that others will also eat from it."

Igwekala laid on his back again and looked at the moon with Obinna. He did not speak for a while. He was thinking about what Obinna had said before he spoke.

"Obinna, I am worried, and I do not understand."

"What do you not understand?

"If the oja creates magic and has these powers that I have witnessed today, why are we looking for help in the east?" he asked. "Why not go back and use it to kill Gandoom and free our people?"

Obinna turned around, looked at him and faced the full moon again without responding.

"Okay, I know, it is the way destiny has planned it, as you said," Igwekala answered his question. He was still not satisfied and sat upright again to ask Obinna more questions.

"You see, a part of me is worried that death could be our destiny; I mean me, you and Ekwueme; a part of me is concerned that the warriors from Tangandoom might win."

Obinna stopped looking at the moon as soon as he said that. He sat upright, looked Igwekala in the eye and placed his hand on his shoulder.

"No. The warriors will not win; they are our audience..." Obinna began to say.

"And this is our stage," Igwekala concluded for him, he had become familiar with that phrase as both men smiled, nodded and slept. As the firewood burnt out through the night, the only sound that could be heard was the birds in the tree, chirping and singing songs with a language which only Obinna understood while he dozed off.

*

The temperature dropped through the night. The men, apart from the drunkard, did not have a good night's sleep as the firewood burnt out quickly. That morning, dry and dusty winds blew against trees, most of which had lost their foliage and the cloudless sky with the peculiar smell of burnt wood indicated that the dry season had kicked in. The evergreen trees which still retained their leaves stood tall and were very visible amongst the sparse vegetation. Several birds had perched on the trees and were chirping loudly.

Obinna was the first to wake up. Igwekala woke up too with a gasp as he was having nightmares through the night and Obinna's body movements disturbed his sleep.

Obinna checked the bag around his waist which had the oja and tapped Ekwueme on the back. He wanted them to carry on with their journey as he did not feel very safe where they were.

He felt a bit hungry and needed a bath.

The drunkard yawned a few times as he stretched himself out, sat upright and rubbed his eyes.

"My head hurts," he complained, "I did not sleep very well."

"No, you slept like a baby; the ground shook while you were snoring," Igwekala informed him.

"We have to carry on with our journey," Obinna suggested, "I am not too sure how long it will take us to get to Kanuri."

"If we walk all day and rest occasionally, we might be able to get there in four days," the drunkard informed them.

He had become sober, and the slur and hiccups had stopped.

"I need to wash," Obinna told the rest.

"There is a river just before Kanuri; we will have to climb a steep hill and get to a bridge built above that river," the drunkard advised them. "The forest that we have to cross before that is fine by me, but I dread that hill," he added, "I am old and not sure if I will have the energy to climb it."

"We can have a bath when we get to the river; I need to wash and dry my garment too," Igwekala said.

The drunkard quickly picked up his wine keg and saw that there was just about enough left.

"Ahh," he said after he slurped the rest of the wine and threw the keg away. "I am ready," he told the others.

So, they walked towards Kanuri. It was not a comfortable journey, but they kept themselves entertained. They knew they had one another and felt safe. The drunkard was like the jester who made them laugh throughout the trip, and he knew it. He felt responsible for them even though he did not care or worry too much about outcomes. He felt like they were his children and needed his guidance. Most of the time, he would overlook their jokes about him but would not hesitate to snap and call them back to order if he felt insulted. When things got a bit heated between him and the rest, he would act silly to make them smile and get them to understand that he did care; at least for them. He was fearless; after all, he was a warrior too, like the rest; Obinna thought so and saw him as one.

Igwekala was the one who asked all the questions and thought things through. He would always advise the rest, but sometimes, it seemed as if he was doubtful and fearful of things he did not understand. He was rational and did not like taking risks. He always had an opinion about the routes, what to eat, or where they should sleep at night. On several occasions, he would try to convince Obinna to teach him how to play the oja. He was inquisitive and liked the melody from the flute, but Obinna would always hesitate and advise him that he might not be ready yet to confront the Omen that followed the bearer of the oja. Obinna knew there was something special about Igwekala; his loyalty and limp made him unique, and he trusted him.

"Limping king," Obinna would praise and call him sometimes when he felt sceptical about things and encouraged him to carry on, and he did.

Obinna was there with them; they trusted and believed in

his magic and knew he could protect them with the oja. They had begun to rely on him totally for every decision they made and would sometimes ask him questions he could not answer.

They would ask him things about the future and reasons certain things happened in the past, and he would try his best to explain but did not have answers to most of those sorts of questions. They refused to believe that Obinna was just a mere human like them.

Igwekala even tried to get him to see the great things they could achieve by harnessing the powers that lie within that flute. He tried to reason with him without causing any offence.

"Obinna, do you realise that what you have is very powerful?" he would ask him. "We do not have to suffer this way."

Obinna would always discourage him from entertaining thoughts about using the oja for any selfish benefits, and he understood.

"I hope I will not have to use the oja to bring death to anyone; rather, I will use it to sustain life and peace," he would always say.

The drunkard was not particularly worried about what the oja could do for them. He felt it was his duty to help his friends. He missed Umuzura and remembered the ill-treatment they all had received at Tangandoom. He wanted revenge and to free the rest of their villagers.

But what the three men had in common was hope. They persevered and believed that somehow, good tends to win over evil. They thought it was the natural order of things.

They felt that all that was happening to them was like a very lengthy and sad song; one that they had no idea when or how it would end.

But however lengthy that song might be, the men had decided that they would dance; not to the tune of their predicament but rather to the magic and melody of the oja.

*

The three of them had journeyed for four days and had arrived in the afternoon, at the hill which the drunkard told them earlier that he dreaded. They stood at the bottom and looked up to see the best way to go over it.

"It is too steep; I will not even make it halfway up," the drunkard lamented.

"We can walk around it, but that will prolong our journey and exhaust you even more," Igwekala informed them.

Obinna gave it a thought and told his friends that they would have to walk over the hill.

"Do not worry," he reassured the drunkard, "there is always a way out of every problem."

He told them to turn their backs to the hill and close their eyes, and they did.

Obinna brought the oja out of his bag, turned his back to the hill with them and played a song. Three steps to the left and three to the right he took as he blew into it. He made a wish with his song and believed with all his heart.

He stopped when he had begun to run out of breath and told his friends to open their eyes and turn around. When they did, they were shocked to see that the hill had disappeared. What stretched out in front of them was a level barren land.

The drunkard could not believe what he was seeing and ran further ahead to where the hill was. He knelt and began to touch the ground as if to check if it was real.

"The hill is gone," he stuttered, "it has vanished completely."

Obinna did not waste much time or marvel at what he had just done. He urged his friends to follow him as he led them through.

The drunkard continued to look in all directions as they walked. He was still searching for where the hill went while Igwekala stared at Obinna with pride.

Igwekala praised Obinna with songs for the rest of the journey. His songs were made up, and all referred to his surprise at what Obinna had turned out to become. The words in his song reminded Obinna of the fact that they had all watched him through the years. They saw him as ordinary; without much prospects, but now revered him and hoped that the powers he had in his possession would help them through their ordeal.

"*My eyes have seen great things happen; no, it was not sorcerers or warriors who did it, it was a young man with the oja; my friend with the oja did it*," he sang.

The men found their way through the forest and got to the footpaths that led to the river. Obinna walked faster. The thought of water made him thirsty, and he began to remove the top part of his garment as they walked.

The sound of the ripples made by the water as it splashed against the riverbank became more audible as they approached.

Obinna was the first to get to the river. He laid his garments down before stepping in bare-chested but still had the oja tied to his waist. He noticed it was immaculate and could see that the river purified itself as it flowed downstream. He looked up and saw the bridge built over it swaying in the wind.

He gestured his friends to join him, and they did. They all removed their clothing, wearing only their undergarments and went to the fastest-flowing part of the river to have a drink.

"The water looks clean and safe to drink here," Igwekala informed them.

"No, wait," Obinna interrupted before they began to drink from the river. "It is not flowing fast enough and might make us sick," he advised.

He brought the oja out from his bag again while his friends watched and blew into it. He began to make ripples in the water with one hand when he stopped playing the flute. As the ripples became more extensive, the men noticed the edges of the ripples illuminate and spread further across the river in circles.

Obinna used the oja to purify the water.

"Now we can drink; I have now cleansed the river," he said as he put the oja back in the bag.

Obinna began to experience flashbacks as he looked in the river. The ripples and the sounds from the river as it washed debris on the bank made him remember Adaure. He began to see her image in the river, but this time, she carried her new-born. The experience felt exactly like the dream he had previously about her; the one when he saw her in the river with her wooden cup filled with olive oil.

Obinna could hear her singing in his head, and it was the same song, *"Love, find me; love, hate me; love, kill me, after all, it is only you; so, love, it is still okay.*"

He felt drawn to her energy when her image in the river reached out and beckoned him to come to her. He did not realise he had begun to submerge himself in the river, knees first, then his entire body followed as though he was in a trance.

He wanted to be with her and let himself go.

Igwekala noticed what had happened when he saw the bag with the oja floating in the river while Obinna was still underwater. He quickly waddled through the river, calling out to him as he approached.

He submerged himself underwater and saw Obinna lying flat on his back at the bottom of the riverbed. He had stopped breathing by the time he got to him.

Igwekala grabbed his arm and pulled him up with all his might. He held Obinna by the waist to keep his head above water, dragged him to the riverbank and laid him down.

The drunkard ran across the river too to meet Igwekala.

"What happened?" he asked, as he and Igwekala panicked while trying to resuscitate Obinna.

"Obinna, wake up; please wake up." They cried and shook his head from side to side.

The drunkard quickly ran back to the river when he saw the oja floating. He got to it on time, picked it up and ran back to where Obinna lay.

He took the oja out of the bag in confusion and began to rub it all over Obinna's head.

"Please wake him up; wake him up," he begged the flute.

"I think he has swallowed some water and cannot breathe properly," Igwekala said.

He held the drunkard's hand to stop him from rubbing the oja all over Obinna and asked him to help turn Obinna around so he could lie on his side. Igwekala could tell his heart was still beating so; he wanted to get rid of some of the water he had swallowed.

Some of the water trickled out of Obinna's mouth as he lay and more came out when Igwekala gave him a pat on the back.

Suddenly, Obinna coughed and shook his head as he began to gasp for air.

"You will be okay; try to relax," both men reassured him as he gradually tried to sit upright.

"What happened?" the drunkard asked him as he secured the oja around Obinna's waist, "You went underwater and refused to come up; were you trying to kill yourself?"

"Tell me what happened, please," Igwekala begged him.

Obinna continued to take deep breathes but replied when he felt a bit better.

"It was Adaure," he told them, "I saw her image in the river, and she asked me to join her."

"Asked you to join her?" the drunkard asked. "Join her where?"

He was puzzled and did not make much sense of Obinna's explanation.

"I was drawn to her energy in the river and did not know that I was sinking; I could not control myself, and before I realised what was going on, I had already gone in, but it felt good; I felt at peace while I was in there."

Igwekala shook his head; he felt sorry for all that his friend had experienced.

"You have suffered, all this happening to us sometimes

makes me wonder what lies ahead; makes me wonder if the price is worth the pain?" he asked.

Obinna got up with a bit of effort and replied:

"Sometimes, pain is what makes us appreciate the price; the price is worthless if there is no pain."

He encouraged his friends not to worry too much and told them to wash their clothes and spread them out to dry before they crossed the bridge with him.

The drunkard informed them as they sat in the sand that since they had walked for four days, the nearest village, Kanuri was not very far off.

Obinna decided that they should continue with their journey. He put his clothes back on, got on the bridge first and held on to its wooden railings as the others climbed up too. He ran his fingers gently over it as he walked on and looked around to enjoy the scenery. The sun was visible in the sky, and the gentle dry wind that blew against his skin gave him a soothing feeling. He liked the way that bridge swayed in the wind as they walked; it gave him a relaxing sensation. Their clothes had not dried completely, but they had to carry on.

Obinna had walked a few steps when he began to experience flashbacks again. He imagined his late father had appeared in the bridge in front of him, he looked worried, and it seemed his father was trying to warn him about something, using hand gestures which he could not quite decipher its meaning. The sense of déjà vu he felt was extreme and similar to the dream he had when he met his father on a bridge, and he stopped abruptly.

Igwekala and the drunkard stopped too when they saw what he had done.

"Is everything okay?" they asked him simultaneously. "Why have you stopped?"

"I do not feel very well," he said. "There is an odd sensation that has just come over me."

"What could it be?" Igwekala asked him, but he did not respond. He stood still on the bridge and stared into the distance. The two men could see that he was looking in the direction of the sun, which was in the sky.

They did not understand why he calmly placed his right hand into his garment as if he was trying to massage the tattoo on his chest.

Obinna pulled his garment down, exposing the tattoo of the rising sun on his chest and would look at it and the sun in the distance over and over again. They had almost forgotten that they had that tattoo drawn on their chests at Tangandoom.

"Leave him alone for a few minutes," Igwekala advised the drunkard, "I think the sun in the sky is reminding him of the tattoo and all our ordeals at Tangandoom."

Igwekala had just finished speaking when Obinna looked up at the sky. They looked up as well to see what caught his attention and what they saw was the parrot, Udele, hovering high above their heads. They did not know that the parrot had been following them and only realised when she appeared from nowhere screaming "Prophecy, prophecy!" as she flew.

Obinna staggered as soon as he heard the parrot and began to lose consciousness.

He quickly tried to reach into his bag for the oja, but it was too late.

Igwekala and the drunkard saw an object fly across the air. It was an arrow that had been shot by someone through the bushes which flew past them and struck Obinna on the chest, just beneath his right shoulder blade. The arrow pierced through him, and the sharp end protruded from his back.

Two more arrows were shot, but they barely missed Igwekala and the drunkard as they fell flat on their backs on the bridge before it got to them.

Obinna looked at his friends, wriggled with pain as he staggered, toppled over the bridge railings and fell into the river.

Igwekala could not bear the pain. The thought that they might have killed his friend shook him. He saw death in Obinna's eyes when he looked at him falling off the bridge, so he got up and jumped into the river with him while the drunkard lay flat on his stomach, pretending to be dead.

Igwekala swam to where Obinna's body floated. The water around them had turned red from the blood that oozed out of his puncture wound. He cried loudly and held Obinna's neck above the surface of the water to prevent him from drowning, but he was careful to avoid being shot at again.

When he scanned through the bushes, he saw six tall women run out from behind trees with bows and arrows. They made unfamiliar sounds with their tongues through the back of their throats as they ran out, which gave the impression that they were ready to fight.

They looked like warriors, and he could understand what they were saying when they spoke to one another. The women looked very strong and muscular, they wore very short garments which hung around their full waists, and they tied the upper part in a notch across their left shoulders. Each one carried a bag full of spare arrows on their backs. They grew their hair in long twists which fell on their backs and were held together by beads made from human teeth, obtained from fallen enemies who they defeated in warfare.

Those women were warriors from Kanuri, the village where they intended to go. They were known as the *Shuri*; females who were born and trained to fight wars and subdue enemies.

They had seen the three men through the bushes as they bathed in the river and patiently waited to understand who the men were and the purpose for which they were there. The Shuri had decided to attack Obinna and his friends when they saw the symbol of the rising sun tattooed on their chests. They were familiar with that symbol and thought that Obinna and his friends were enemies from Tangandoom. The Shuri knew that only the warriors from Tangandoom had those tattoos.

Many years ago, Gandoom and his executioner had besieged Kanuri and had forcefully seized almost all their livestock and taken some prisoners with them. Their king, Nuri survived the siege with the help of the female warriors and ever since then, their village had become extremely cautious with regards to their security.

"Seize the enemy on the bridge, and I will take care of these two," one of the women commanded.

The Shuri did as she was told and went up the bridge to get the drunkard who had gotten up quickly and attempted to flee, but she subdued him.

Igwekala panicked, as two of them approached him in the water and began to plead for mercy.

"Please spare us; we do not mean any harm; please do

not harm us."

His pleas fell on deaf ears as the Shuri who had authority over the rest struck him on the head with a blunt weapon which dazed him, and he passed out too.

They were all dragged to the riverbank and tied up.

"These are those dogs from Tangandoom," one of them said as she inspected the tattoos on their chests again.

"There is no need for further delay, let me cut their hearts out now and throw them in the river," another one snarled.

"No, we should take them back alive for questioning," their leader interrupted. "If that evil king, Gandoom has sent them here, he must have a reason; we need to interrogate them and find out what his plan is."

"This one probably will not make it alive as he has lost a lot of blood," one said, referring to Obinna, who was not moving at all.

Their leader looked at Obinna, bent over and broke the sharp end of the arrow protruding from his back. She asked the rest to hold him down, and she quickly pulled the arrow out from his wound.

The drunkard grimaced when she pulled it out, but Obinna did not move at all.

She carefully observed him where he lay and saw the bag tied around his waist. The Shuri opened the bag and brought out the oja, looked at it properly and decided to keep it for herself.

The drunkard became nervous when she took the oja from Obinna. He felt that they would become powerless without it and that their lives would be in great danger.

Obinna's wound was tied up with a cloth to stop the

bleeding.

"The horses will carry them; the rest of you, search the area and make sure they are the only ones here," she ordered.

Three of the Shuri lifted them on their shoulders quickly, got on the bridge and walked to where their horses were grazing. They laid each man on a horse and held the leash as they took them back to Kanuri, which was not far off.

*

They had almost reached the entrance to the village in the evening.

The drunkard kept his eyes open throughout the journey. He would not risk sleeping because he was terrified. The leader of the Shuri was the one who led the horse on which they tied him. He had tried to engage her in a conversation during the journey, but she refused to speak to him. The drunkard sensed that she somewhat found him odd but intriguing.

She did not like the idea of being asked personal questions about anything by an enemy, but the drunkard persisted.

"How are you feeling?" he asked her. "You must be exhausted carrying all those heavy arrows on your back." He talked to her as if he cared.

She looked at him angrily but did not respond and led the horse along.

The drunkard tried to sit upright and adjust himself as his hands were tied.

"Stay where you are," she warned him. "If you fall off this horse, I will leave you tied on the ground for the vultures to eat your flesh."

"I will be fine with the vultures," the drunkard replied. "They will spare my life when they see that I have been dropped off by you; the most powerful, elegant and beautiful female warrior my eyes will probably ever see," he teased.

The Shuri looked at him from the corner of her eyes and carried on walking.

The drunkard did not stop. He persisted with his conversation and hoped she might begin to respond.

"So, tell me, have you been a warrior all your life?" he asked her. "We have female warriors called the Idanuwo in our village too, but they look nothing like you; you stand out."

She hesitated a bit but responded very firmly,

"I have been a warrior long enough to recognise you filthy dogs from Tangandoom who prowl the earth looking for people to devour and blood to spill."

"No, we are not really who you think we are," he denied. "We are not from Tangandoom," he stuttered. "Sorry, I meant we are from there; that is where we are coming from, but we are not really from there." The drunkard struggled to explain himself as he was nervous.

"Do you understand?" he asked her.

She did not speak nor look at him, and he threw in another question.

"I am only asking because I can see that dreadful scar on your neck," he referred to an injury she had sustained on her neck which had healed but left terrible marks which were only visible when her hair parted to the side.

"How did you get that scar? From killing innocent people like me?" he joked.

The Shuri turned and looked at him with rage, reached out and dragged him down from the horse like a weightless object, slammed him on the ground and quickly pulled out an arrow from the bag behind her back. She held the shaft against his neck while breathing heavily.

The rest stopped to see what was going on.

"I will say this once and never again; do not ever refer to my scar or anything in particular that has got to do with me," she warned. "Do you hear me?"

"Yes, I did, and I am sorry," he replied, realising that what he said had struck a nerve. He did not speak to her any further but continued to wonder why his comment had infuriated her in that way.

She picked him up roughly again and threw him on the horse's back and ordered the rest to move.

They arrived at a canal which the Shuri dug to protect the village from intruders. The only way to cross was by canoe. The Shuri warriors built that canal to serve as an ambush for intruders who intend to attack their village and the idea behind constructing it was that any intruder who tried to gain unauthorised access to the village would have no choice but to try and go around it. The Shuri would then ambush any such person at both ends of the canal.

The canoes were already waiting at the dock near the edge of the canal to pick up the warriors. They lifted Obinna and his friends from the horses, and they all got on the canoes. Igwekala and the Shuri got in on the same canoe. It seemed she put him on her boat on purpose. Obinna and Igwekala were each put on separate ones, each driven by one of the warriors.

The drunkard had been observing her throughout the

journey. He felt that the responsibility was upon him to try and find a solution to their predicament. He believed he was the voice that needed to speak up to save his friends and had noticed something unique with the Shuri each time she finished speaking. Her head would slightly tilt to the side, followed by a shoulder twitch. He had also noticed that she had figured out a way not to make it look apparent. He thought that if he could somehow win her trust, perhaps it would work in their favour at Kanuri.

Besides, he liked her and wanted to try and get to know her better; he was willing to look for love amid hatred, so, he spoke to her again on the canoe as they rode along.

"Your twitch," he said. "The thing you do with your head and shoulder after you speak—" he mimicked her head movement "—my friend on that boat can make it go away; he is a magician."

He paused to let her think through his suggestion and was carefully observing her reaction.

The Shuri looked right into the drunkard's eyes for a few seconds and looked across at the boats that carried Obinna and Igwekala but remained silent as she looked away. She began to paddle the canoe a lot faster than before.

"Please trust me, he can," he continued, "but you will have to give him back that flute in the bag you took from him," he said, pointing at Obinna's oja which she had already tied around her waist.

"It is his source of magic; he cannot help you without it, and something terrible might happen to us if you don't give it back to him."

They rowed the canoes to the edge of the canal where they docked them, and the Shuri got out first.

The drunkard could see the entrance gate to the village further ahead as he was dragged out from the canoe. More Shuri ran over to them and carried the injured men on their shoulders towards the entrance. One tried to take the drunkard too but was interrupted.

"No, I will take this one in myself."

*

They were greeted at the entrance gate to Kanuri by the rest of the Shuri who stood guard waiting for them. As they laid Obinna and Igwekala on the floor, the Shuri who led them informed the others to bring some bamboo stretchers and carry the two wounded men. Igwekala regained consciousness and began to mumble Obinna's name as he opened his eyes, but the Shuri told him to remain quiet as they were carried in. The drunkard walked alongside their leader and began to speak to her again.

"Please think about what I told you earlier on that canoe," he requested, "you will not regret it."

"I have thought about whatever it is you said already," she replied, "I do not need your help."

They opened the entrance gates, and they went in. The drunkard looked around, and all he could see were palm trees. He could not count them as they were too many. Their stems were beautified with ornaments, and some were even painted in different colours. It seemed they used the trees only for decoration and some served as sheds from the direct heat of the sun as wooden chairs were arranged underneath them. He saw signs hanging on a few of the trees which read: '*The gardens of pleasure*,' and smiled. He understood what

179

pleasure meant and the feelings associated with it, but to him, he only felt it when he was inebriated.

An overpowering smell filled the air as they carried on. The drunkard thought the scent was goat meat burned over a fire and as they walked through the garden, he was amazed when they arrived at an open space spanning almost four thousand feet across the middle. He had calculated the size of the land by estimating that it was at least twenty-five times the size of their arena at Umuzura where they held the Udunre festival. That land was where the villagers reared the livestock for which they were famous. Paddocks, fences and shelters were built within that space to house the animals.

"There is more livestock here than people in my village," he said to the Shuri as he looked around. He could see very busy farmers. Some fed cattle, while others prepared the grains used to produce the food the animals ate. Some tradesmen were busy isolating some animals in cages to be transported for sale, and he could see what looked like a slaughterhouse where they prepared meat. There was a lot of noise from the animals. Goats and sheep bleated, horses neighed, and monkeys chattered; it made the drunkard feel as though he was in the middle of a bustling market.

"Your village must be rich," he said. "You must be making a lot of money from these animals after sales."

The Shuri instructed the rest to carry Obinna and Igwekala away, revive and treat them so she could go and have a word with Nuri, their king. The drunkard tried to follow her further, but she declined.

"You will wait here," she firmly said and beckoned another warrior over to take him away before she proceeded.

*

The sun had fully set when she arrived at the king's palace. They had already set the tables for his meal, and several servants were busy with chores when she entered. She first removed the arrows she was carrying and handed them, with her bow, to someone at the door as a sign of respect to the king. At Kanuri, they took their meals and wine seriously and saw merriment as rituals which humans must perform to appreciate life. Each time they ate, they enjoyed it as if it would be their last meal. They would sing first, dance and hug themselves before eating. Even some of their animals were invited to the party. She got there on time for the celebration and was ushered in by a woman who wore beads around her waist and arms. The woman held her by the hand, smiling and dancing.

"My Shuri; great protector of Kanuri, welcome," the woman greeted her. "You have arrived just at the right time; they have set the tables, and the king is in there."

"I appreciate your hospitality," she replied with a smile. "May the gods strengthen your hips so that you will continue to dance here and in the afterlife."

"We are serving pounded yam, pepper soup, rice and *uha* vegetables plus snail and spices," she informed her.

"Ah, my mouth is already watering, and I cannot wait to devour what they have cooked," the Shuri replied with a smile, parted the curtains that led into the palace and walked in.

The king was already on his feet, dancing to the music the drummers were playing. It seemed he had already had a bit too much to drink and was very merry that evening. He would spread his robes with both hands, spin around and sing with others who were present there at the dinner table.

"Shuri, the strongest and fairest of them all, welcome to our celebration of life," he turned around and praised her when he saw her walk in. "You look a bit worried and stressed, come and join us; the music the drummers are playing is: '*The curse that gave us blessings*' and the flautists are playing: '*Tomorrow is today*,'" he said. "Come, join me; let us dance and let tomorrow worry about itself."

She hesitated a bit but smiled, joined the king and danced very briefly with him before stopping.

Nuri looked at her and slowed down. He could see that something was bothering her, so he informed the drummers and flautists to stop playing so they could eat.

"What seems to be the problem?" he asked her as he sat down with everyone else in the palace. The king would usually wash his hands in a bowl of water placed at the centre of the table, talk to everyone about the state of affairs in their village briefly before they began to eat, but he did not speak to them after washing his hands. He wanted an immediate response. The king highly respected the Shuri. She was the highest-ranked warrior in the village and commanded the rest of the female warriors. She and her troops bore the entire responsibility of protecting the king and the village. Whenever she spoke, the king listened very attentively.

"My king, may you live forever," she greeted him at the table. "Some bad and old memories have returned and besieged us; somehow, I knew this day would come," she complained.

"What memories do you speak of?" Nuri asked. "Tell me exactly what the problem is."

"My king, my warriors and I found three intruders at the river; I think they are warriors or spies from Tangandoom; I saw the tattoos on their chests."

The king froze with fear when he heard her mention Tangandoom. Their village had a horrible experience many years ago when King Gandoom sent his executioner and warriors to invade them. A battle broke out, but Nuri lost the war. Their village lost many warriors in that battle; the invaders took most of their livestock as well as many prisoners. Nuri escaped and survived the war, but after that ordeal, they felt the loss they suffered for many years. It took them a while to rebuild their village and make up for what was lost. During that war, the Shuri had a personal encounter with Gandoom's executioner; the executioner killed her father who was Nuri's most potent warrior at that time, she survived but had sustained the injury on her neck from the executioner's sword. The mental trauma and injury resulted in her epileptic seizures and muscle twitches whenever she was stressed, but she had grown and decided to put the thoughts behind her and carry on. She had vowed to avenge her father's death someday, so began to train fearlessly in the art of warfare as the years went by. Her passion, hope and strength burnt within her like fire, and she had mastered how to use bows and arrows as well as how to subdue an enemy physically. She stood out amongst the rest and recruited women to become warriors like herself. She was the one that gave them the name: Shuri, a title she preferred to be called by as she had given up her birth name. She also trained them to become as fierce and strong as she was.

The king dropped his cutlery on the table, stood up and walked away. Everyone in the palace could see he was worried.

"So Gandoom has remembered us again?" he asked. "Has he not had enough?" He shook his head in disapproval, walked back to the table and sat down.

"Where are these intruders now?" he asked. "If they are alive, you must bring them to me for questioning; we must find out what their next plan is so we can counter their offence before they attack us."

"We captured three of them, and we have taken them to the medicine chambers for treatment," she replied. "I will bring them to you tomorrow if they are well enough to speak."

The king held his head with both hands and looked downwards at the table. He silently cried as the news had brought back sad memories of the previous war. He did not want to risk the lives of his people but did not know what to do or when to do it.

The Shuri got up from her seat and walked over to the king. She knelt next to him and held his knee with one arm to reassure him that she was still loyal and dedicated in her service to the village.

"My king, do not worry, I took a vow to serve you and protect this village; I have lived by that promise and want to let you know that I would not live to see anyone hurt you or anybody from our village; Kanuri will live forever, and I will do all that is within my power to ensure that we are safe."

Her shoulder muscles began to twitch as she convulsed with her neck tilted to the side, while she maintained eye contact with the king.

"Oh, you have suffered much violence, my Shuri," he replied, rubbing her shoulders with his palm to calm her down. "You were such a young girl when they killed your father, and I have watched you grow into this strong, loyal woman that you are now," he continued. "I know your twitches bring back bad memories, but I believe one day, you will be well again."

She began to relax as the seizures gradually wore off, stood up and replied:

"My king, some memories vanish with time while some others are destined to linger."

Dinner that night was not how it used to be. They all sat and ate as they passed plates of food to one another. There was not much to discuss as everyone thought about the information they had just received. The drummers stopped, but the flautists changed the music to something more mellow to help everyone relax as they ate. Often, someone would smile and say something to lighten the mood, but their worries lingered throughout dinner till they finished.

The Shuri thanked the king, got up and secured Obinna's flute, which she tied around her waist and informed the king she was about to leave.

"I will go and check if our sorcerer has been able to treat the intruders," she said. "Tomorrow, by midday, I will bring them to you for questioning," she concluded, parted the curtains and walked out. She took her bow and arrows at the door from the person who held it for her and walked out into the night.

The night was tranquil. It seemed all the animals had gone to sleep rather unusually early. All she heard as she walked along was the sound of birds chirping in the distance and a parrot saying "Prophecy, prophecy," repetitively from where she perched high above her head. That parrot was

Udele; she was there at Kanuri. She looked up to see where the sound came from but saw nothing so, she carried on walking and tried her best to appreciate the beauty of the moon that illuminated the night sky.

*

She did not go home but went straight to the medicine chambers where they treated injured people. She wanted to see if they had revived the intruders. She thought briefly about what the drunkard had told her on the canoe but tried to distract herself with other thoughts. The king's sorcerer was already there when she walked in. The sorcerer was the one responsible for treating injuries and giving the king advice regarding things the ordinary eyes could not see or comprehend. He had supernatural gifts, and the village found him very useful. He understood magic like Obinna but was more specialised in herbal medicine and had psychic abilities.

She looked around and saw the sorcerer walking around Obinna in circles where he lay. Igwekala and the drunkard sat next to each other. Obinna was still unconscious, and she could see that the sorcerer was mixing a condiment of herbs in a cup. He dipped his finger in the mixture and let it drop onto Obinna's forehead.

"I hope this will open his third eye and will be a channel for good energies to pass through him and make him well again," the sorcerer told her. "He is badly hurt and has lost a lot of blood; I do not know if he will make it at all."

Igwekala began to cry when he heard what the sorcerer said, and the drunkard held his hands to console him.

"You will have to give him back that flute; please, he will die if you do not; terrible things will happen if you refuse, please," he begged the Shuri. "Why have you taken what belongs to him?" he asked her. "It is not fair."

The Shuri became enraged with what the drunkard said. She ran towards him, pulled him up by the garment and replied:

"Did you say I took what belongs to him?" she asked angrily. "A useless flute?" she asked again. "Is that what I took from him?"

Her shoulder began to twitch again as she spoke, and the drunkard could see her eyes turn red.

She was crying while she challenged him.

"Do you know what you people have taken from me?" she sobbed. "My father, my life; everything."

She let go of the drunkard and staggered backwards. Her anger had taken over her emotions, and she began to act confused.

"You took it all, and now I am cursed," she lamented. "But you know what?" she continued, "I have embraced my curse and woe betide anybody who dares stand in the way of my vengeance; I will not rest until I see the earth open up and swallow Gandoom and that executioner of his."

"Shuri," the drunkard called her, "we are all cursed, and I am sorry for your loss."

He walked a bit closer but not too close in case she lost her temper again:

"You have my word that I will help you smile again," he said, "If you trust me, we will break the curse, and it will all be a story that will be told to future generations to come."

"They will meet the king tomorrow at midday," she

informed the sorcerer. "If you cannot revive that one, leave him to die and let his friends speak up and explain what their purpose in our village is."

She walked out from the room and left the sorcerer there who stood up and continued looking at Obinna where he lay.

"Do you think he will survive?" Igwekala asked the sorcerer.

"That is not important now," he replied, "I have inserted a tube into the vein in his right arm through which we can feed him, tomorrow, you will have to explain yourselves to the king, and if you have come to us with hate, destiny will decide what will happen to you eventually."

"But we are not warriors from Tangandoom; we were prisoners there," the drunkard explained. "We are telling you the truth."

"Then speak for yourselves tomorrow; I will be there to listen," and he left the room.

"That man looks very different; he looks like a foreigner," the drunkard said, referring to the sorcerer.

Igwekala and the drunkard could see that Obinna's health was not improving. They did not realise that he had gone into a partial comatose state. His heart was still beating, and he was breathing very slightly but had lost all sensory functions and was unaware of his immediate environment. The drunkard sat next to him and held his hands while Igwekala placed his head on his lap.

"I am tired," Igwekala told the drunkard. "We are going to lose Obinna, and I have not got any more energy left in me to bear all this; I give up."

"No, Igwekala, what has become of you?" the drunkard asked him. "Where are your hope and morale?" he asked.

"You have been the one constantly telling me about self-improvement, about right and wrong; now listen to yourself; you sound hopeless," he cautioned him. "Most of my life, I have not cared much about anything other than wine, but now I have the opportunity to right my wrong; to break my curse, and all you can do is give up?" he asked. "You can sit there and cry in defeat, but me? I will drink again; this time not from the cup of hopelessness, but the cup of victory," he insisted. "I will find a way to help, and I do not know how."

Igwekala pulled himself together and nodded in agreement to what the drunkard said.

"And may I just add; I am in love with that Shuri, and I am going to sweep her off her feet, you just wait and see," the drunkard said with a wink.

Igwekala smiled at the ridiculous statement the drunkard had just made. He knew it was impossible but was used to his effronteries.

That night they slept, holding Obinna's hands and hoped the next day would not be their last.

*

The Shuri got to the medicine chamber at midday, as planned with two others. She informed them to bring Igwekala and the drunkard to the king's palace but asked that they leave Obinna behind as he was still unconscious. She felt that there would be no need to take him along because he would not be able to speak up for himself. Whatever judgement the king passed upon the others would have to be his as well.

The drunkard was not pleased with that decision and begged the Shuri to allow Obinna to be present at the palace too.

"Please bring him along, he has been running with us, and it would be unfair to leave him behind in the middle of the race."

The Shuri agreed, and the three others went out, came back in with a bamboo stretcher with which they picked Obinna up. One tried to tie Igwekala, and the drunkard's hands behind their backs but the Shuri told her not to as they were escorted out.

King Nuri was already waiting in the palace with the sorcerer, a few palace workers and some more warriors when they entered. Some people started murmuring as they laid Obinna's stretcher on the ground. A few others pointed fingers, and the drunkard could see angry faces staring at them. He felt they were in the wrong place at the wrong time.

The king did not waste much time; he stood up first and spoke.

"Shuri, greetings to you on behalf of Kanuri," he recognised her first. "Who are these you have brought to me today and for what purpose?"

"My king, they are the intruders from Tangandoom, we captured at the river; I have brought them here for questioning and judgement."

The king walked a bit closer to them with a disgusted look on his face and spoke.

"Tangandoom, when will your thirst for blood cease?" he asked them. "You won the previous war, so what is your interest in our peaceful village again?"

"We are not from Tangandoom," the drunkard spoke up quickly. "We were held there as prisoners."

"Yes, we are from Umuzura; the village on the east from

190

Kanuri, King Gandoom attacked our village during our festival and took many of our villagers as prisoners," Igwekala added.

"We suffered there; oh, we suffered, too much work," the drunkard stuttered. "We almost gave up hope."

"But something happened," Igwekala chimed in,

"Yes, something magical," the drunkard added.

"A flute set us free; our friend's oja saved us," Igwekala replied, pointing at Obinna where he lay.

"But they are still holding our people there as prisoners."

"As well as the love of his life; Adaure and her new-born,"

"You will find it difficult to believe, but it is true," the drunkard cut in again,

"And all this happened because of a curse; a curse from a parrot called Udele." The drunkard frowned as he shook his head.

The king ran out of patience with their prolonged story and had to cut it short.

"Shut up," he ordered. "I have heard enough of this cock-and-bull story."

He turned over to the Shuri and requested for any evidence that linked them to their suspicions of where they came from, and she replied:

"My king, they bear the tattoo of the rising sun on their chests like the rest of them." She walked over to Igwekala and pulled down his top garment to show the king.

The drunkard noticed that the Shuri refused to make eye contact with him throughout the interrogation. He was not entirely sure as to the reason why, but a part of him thought that she felt a bit sorry for what the outcome of that hearing would be.

The king looked at both men, at the Shuri and quickly turned his back on them.

"I will ask you just this once and if you cooperate, I might temper justice with mercy, so, what is your king's next plan for us?" he asked. "You must tell me when or how he intends to wage the next war so we will prepare for it."

The drunkard spoke before Igwekala could respond:

"We are not from Tangandoom, it is the truth, and we know nothing of their king's secrets."

The king did not hesitate any further. He had already made up his mind. He had quickly thought of the suffering that the previous war brought upon his people and felt that this was a way to pay Tangandoom back for their evil, so, he passed his judgement.

"The elephant that topples everything over with rage will understand fear the day it meets the helpless mouse," he concluded. "Throw these evil men to the alligators now and watch them till they eat the last flesh from their bones; this is our revenge; this is my justice."

The drunkard and Igwekala fell on their knees pleading for mercy as three of the Shuri approached and seized them. Two picked up the stretcher on which Obinna lay and carried him up but again their leader refused to participate. There seemed to be something troubling her mind. Even though she was satisfied with the fate of her enemies, a part of her felt that the time was not quite right, or was she being carried away by her emotions? She thought.

There was no time left to think. The king's justice had been served, and she had to act upon it. They seized the men, and as they were being marched out from the palace, someone spoke up and interrupted them.

"Wait!" the voice said, and everyone looked over to see who it was.

It was the king's sorcerer. He had remained silent throughout the interrogation but had decided to speak up.

"My king, may I please ask that they lay that prisoner down, his friends have spoken, but he needs to speak; we have not heard from him," he said, referring to Obinna.

"He cannot speak, he is not awake, so how is that possible, sorcerer?" the king asked as the Shuri who carried him waited at the door.

"It is possible with magic," the sorcerer replied. "The physical is flawed; it can deceive because it only understands self-preservation but the soul never lies, it will tell us the truth that we need to hear."

The king agreed to his sorcerer's request and asked them to bring Obinna and his friends back to the centre of the room. He was laid down, and the sorcerer pulled up the white garment he wore, which swept the ground and walked over to where he lay. He knelt next to him, bent over with his eyes closed and began to touch Obinna's cheeks as he stared into his closed eyelids.

"Earth, wind, water and fire," he said as he slowly moved his fingers down Obinna's neck and shoulders till he held his hands. "Come together and awaken the soul of the one who needs to be heard."

A gust of wind blew through the palace as the ground shook. The sorcerer saw tears trickle down the side of Obinna's eyes and his hands felt warm.

The sorcerer stood back as Obinna's soul rose from his physical body, which lay on the ground. Everyone, including the king, could see it, and they all screamed with fear.

The drunkard and Igwekala were shocked but quite pleased to see Obinna as he stood there. He had a very solemn look on his face and seemed a bit confused. They all could see a bright light that encircled him where he stood, and when he spoke, his voice echoed in the room.

Obinna looked down and saw his lifeless body on the stretcher, looked around the room and spoke to Igwekala first.

"Igwekala, am I dead?" he asked.

"No, you are not," Igwekala replied.

"Where is Adaure?" he asked.

"They are still in Tangandoom with your baby."

"Obinna, it is nice to see you this way again," the drunkard said.

Obinna smiled at him as he continued looking around, trying to remember where he was and how he got there.

"What am I doing here?" he asked.

"I summoned you," the sorcerer interrupted.

"And why have you done so?"

"Because I have a feeling, it is your destiny as well as mine," the sorcerer replied.

Obinna paused, thought about it for a moment...

"Or could it be that you want me to tell you something?" Obinna asked.

"Hm, something like what?" the sorcerer wondered.

"The truth that my friends have told you all along that we are not from Tangandoom; we are prisoners from there, or is there something else you wanted to hear?"

"Ah, we both know the first truth is correct and is what we wanted to hear, after all, we are both meant to be the magicians aren't, we?" the sorcerer replied.

"What sort of magic found you?" Obinna asked him.

"Nature; the sort that falls from the skies when it gets freezing," he replied.

"I come from a land, far away, where magic could be felt even in the cold when ice crystals fall from the skies.

"Ice crystals from the skies?" Obinna wondered. "Where is this land, and what do those crystals look like?"

"It is a country called England and those crystals we refer to as snow; I will show you but tell me first, what did that prison at Tangandoom look or feel like?"

"It felt terrible at first, but later it began to feel as if it was normal; as if I needed to be there; they covered the walls with messages, but one particular note saved my life; it read *'To find your way out, you must first find your way in.'*"

"For the keys that you seek are with and within you," the sorcerer replied before he could finish.

Obinna looked at him with shock, his jaw dropped, and he asked:

"So, it was you; you wrote the message on the prison's wall?"

"Yes, I did, and I never thought I would live to see the day I would come face to face with whom it was intended for; whom it would help," the sorcerer agreed.

"Thank you; you saved my life," Obinna replied.

"No, you saved mine," the sorcerer corrected. "You gave my life meaning and purpose."

"How?" Obinna asked,

"Gandoom's magician, Suleiman, helped me to find my magic when I was held there as a prisoner and told me that if I agreed to help someone, the one who also needs to find his,

I would escape, through the powers of magic; that one is you."

Obinna continued to listen.

"When they imprisoned me there, I continued to have these nightmares; I kept seeing a bird that wanted to hurt me; Suleiman helped me to realise who I was and one day, I woke up and saw myself outside of their prison walls; that was how I escaped." The sorcerer explained.

"Suleiman is dead; they killed him," Obinna revealed.

The sorcerer looked away, hiding tears when he heard about what happened to Suleiman but continued.

"I first came here from England as a young missionary to spread a certain message, during my stay here, this village got attacked, and I was taken as prisoner and kept within those walls at Tangandoom. Then Suleiman came to me and showed me who I was; he helped me vanish through those walls and told me that I would have to guide someone else. I left that message for you."

Both men stopped speaking for a while as everyone in the palace paid keen attention.

"What about you?" the sorcerer asked Obinna. "What sort of magic found you?

"The oja; my flute," he replied. "It has a voice, and when it speaks, everything has no choice but to listen."

"We are listening; tell us, what does it have to say? We are your audience, and this is your stage," the sorcerer replied.

Obinna knew the oja was not with him. He saw it glowing as it hung on the Shuri's waist, and he walked over to her. She froze with fear and hesitated as he reached for the flute, but the drunkard reassured her that all is well.

"Let him have it; it is a part of him."

Obinna's soul reached out and took the oja. He took the flute, but they could still see it hanging on the Shuri's waist.

It seemed the oja had a soul of its own and Obinna was in its possession. Three steps to left and three to the right he took and played a song for them.

The sorcerer joined Obinna's dance. He too conjured magic as they both swayed around the room to his melody. That afternoon, it snowed indoors, inside the palace while they danced. It did not take long for the king, the Shuri, Igwekala and the drunkard to join them as they became mesmerised by the music. They had never seen snow before and marvelled as pure white crystals fell through the roof and drenched them but quickly disappeared as they hit the ground.

Obinna spoke to all of them with the oja that day.

To the Shuri, he opened her eyes and showed her a garden filled with roses and in that garden was the drunkard. He pleaded with her to give love a chance; to fight for it like the warrior she was. He told her that her twitch would never return because the drunkard wished it so.

To Igwekala, he thanked him for his loyalty and once again called him 'The limping king.'

He whispered in King Nuri's ears and told him that the drunkard had a secret to prosperity he would reveal to him and also encouraged him to rule his people with integrity.

To the drunkard, he told him to show the king how to tap palm wine from the palm trees in the gardens of pleasure. He informed him to make the king aware that he could maximise his profit if he utilised those palm trees not just for decoration but for its primary purpose, which is wine.

He told the sorcerer that he would have to go back to

England eventually because his missionary work was not yet complete. He made him aware that there are millions more all over the world with gifts; people who possess the magic they have been searching for but need help to find it, he told the sorcerer that it was his duty to look for them, one magician at a time, till he finds them all and then will the world know peace.

And he ended his song as his soul went back into his sick body and vanished. The oja became one again with that which the Shuri tied to her waist, and the snow stopped.

They all found it challenging to speak afterwards. The experience was very intense as everyone gasped for air.

King Nuri broke the silence and spoke first.

"Friends, my eyes have seen wonders today, pick the sick one up and take these innocent men to the fattening chambers, give them everything they want; food, wine, medicine for they are one of us now."

The Shuri looked at the drunkard, smiled, and he smiled back at her. She walked over to where Obinna lay first, untied the oja from her waist and tied it around his, then walked towards the drunkard and took his hand. Obinna's stretcher was picked up, and they carried them out to be looked after as the king requested. But before they left, the king spoke to the drunkard and asked him a question.

"Isn't there meant to be a secret you should share with me?" he said with a big smile on his face.

"Yes, my king," the drunkard replied, "I need to show you the way to a man's heart." They all laughed as he, the Shuri, the sorcerer and the king walked out from the palace together with Igwekala limping alongside them. They all headed towards the gardens of pleasure, where they grew the palm trees.

Chapter Five

One year had passed at Kanuri. The rainy season had returned, and King Nuri and his people had become extremely wealthy from the sale of palm wine to other villages. They had perfected ways to cultivate the trees and nurture them as the drunkard showed them. The village did not have to rely solely on the sale of their livestock to make ends meet. Their business was booming, and their community had become the envy of their neighbours.

Nuri made the drunkard and Igwekala royals and gave them many servants to tend to their needs. He also gave the drunkard authority and ownership to half of his palm tree plantations and the wine that they produced from it.

"They say sometimes wishes do come true," the drunkard would often tell Igwekala when they were alone. He would remind him of that day that he blew into Obinna's flute and wished for a river of wine. He would insist that his wishes did come true; that he got more than a river; an endless supply of wine in the form of palm trees, given to him by their friend Nuri.

The drunkard and the Shuri had become partners and had fallen in love. She would often tell him that there were only two things she could have possibly done with him which were to either kill him or love him and he would reply,

"My love, I was already dead before I saw you, but after I met you, I felt alive again."

Igwekala continued to grieve over Obinna who was still in a partial state of coma. He shaved off all the hair on his head and refused to trim his whiskers. He convinced the king to build a pedestal in a separate room on which they laid Obinna's sleeping body upon and the villagers would go there every week to meditate. His body became an oracle where they went to cleanse their minds and purify themselves. He believed that someday, his friend would wake up. They had previously tried to talk to the king about the possibilities of going to war with Gandoom, to free Adaure and the rest of their villagers in captivity, but the king reminded them that war was too risky and that they all might not live through it. So, they had begun to live their lives as usual at Kanuri.

The sorcerer had informed the king that he would be going back to England by sea in a month and the king promised to build him a vessel he would use to sail home. He felt that his time at Kanuri was complete. He had shown them how to keep Obinna fed through the tube inserted in his vein. He did not summon Obinna's soul again but left him alone to sleep in peace.

"Let him sleep," he would say to the king. "He is living out a curse; if the curse is broken, he will rise again."

*

Obinna did not wake up as he expected. Little did they realise that at Tangandoom, the evil king, Gandoom and his executioner had planned a final assault. They had several meetings, and the king had decided that they would have to seize the oja, but firstly Obinna must be captured. They wanted to harness the power within the flute to make their village a potent force. They intended to use Obinna and the oja as a weapon to conquer all territories far and near. The memories of what happened the day that Obinna and his two friends walked away from captivity was still fresh in the king's mind, but he and the executioner had been too shaken to think about war. They agreed that the time to act had arrived and there was no need for further delay.

Gandoom sent twelve of his strongest warriors and his executioner to journey to the east and west to find where Obinna was hiding and summon whoever he was with to hand him over, otherwise, face destruction, and they set out on that journey as instructed.

And the warriors did find where Obinna and his friends were. They had arrived at the canal on their horses trying to figure out how to go around it before being ambushed by the Shuri.

"We are warriors of the rising sun from the north; King Gandoom has given his order that you hand over the one that bears the flute immediately or face death and destruction," the executioner demanded.

The leader of the Shuri thought quickly and informed her warriors not to respond with hostility. She was considering the possibility of deescalating the situation. She knew that Gandoom's army was more powerful than hers and that they would lose terribly in a war.

She emerged, stood in front of the executioner and replied:

"Go back to your village, the one who bears the flute is

202

not your property."

The executioner dismounted his horse when he saw her. He walked over steadily but majestically and looked closely at the scar on her neck. He remembered who she was and knew that he was the one that gave her that scar and said:

"I know you; if revenge is what you seek, you will have to count every single sand in the desert first before you find it," he snarled.

The Shuri replied:

"The sands in the desert will give me justice when they swallow you and your king up, never to be seen again."

"I will return in seven days, and if you do not hand him over before then, I will have a special gift for you," he growled.

The warriors from Tangandoom stormed off on their horses.

*

King Nuri was made aware of what happened at the canal, and he became worried. He summoned a meeting immediately to discuss the next plan. Handing Obinna over to the enemy was not an option because they felt it would be a betrayal. They had bonded with him and his friends. He asked his sorcerer for advice, but he shook his head and replied:

"My king, you cannot change the course of destiny; I have fully prepared for how it will all end."

That meeting was not very productive. The king had to adjourn it for the next day as they had not come up with any reasonable plan to avert the calamity that would befall them.

Everyone left the palace and went home, apart from the Shuri. She refused to go with the drunkard.

"Go, my love, I need to speak to Obinna; there is something I must tell him," she said.

That night, she went to the pedestal where he was laid alone and informed others that she needed to be in there all by herself.

When she got in, she first checked the tube inserted in his vein to make sure it was still in place. She took a piece of cloth, dipped it in a water bowl near the pedestal and wiped his face with it. As she adjusted the white garment with which they wrapped him up, she began to cry.

"You will never wake up, will you?" she asked him. "They said you are living out a curse, but exactly how long will your curse last?"

She reminded Obinna about how far he had come, about what the drunkard had told her that they had experienced.

"You cannot give up now; if you do, your curse then wins," she cried.

She reminded him about the oja and the magic it possessed and the fact that nobody else could use it to help them apart from him.

"What about Adaure?" she asked. "Have you ever wondered if she is still alive?"

She reminded Obinna of the fact that the warriors at Tangandoom might have killed her and the new-born. She held his cheeks and apologised because she felt that it was her arrow that was responsible for putting him in the coma.

"Do you hear me, Obinna?" she cried and began to lose her temper when she realised that she was only talking to herself.

"No, you do not care; you just want to be left alone in peace so you can sleep."

She began to shake Obinna's head violently, hitting his chest where he lay with all her might as she cried, "Wake up, wake up now, I say."

Someone rushed in and grabbed her hands from behind to stop her. It was the drunkard. He had followed her shortly after she went in and had to intervene when her emotions flared up.

"Please calm down; everything will be okay," he said as he gently escorted her out.

"Everything will be okay at the right time."

*

The seventh day had arrived. The entire village at Kanuri woke up very early as nobody slept adequately through the night. Igwekala and the drunkard went to the room where they laid Obinna and sat there with him. They refused to leave his side. They had made up their minds that they would be there with him till the end even if they all had to die from the warrior's swords that day. They were not sure what the warriors would do if they did return.

The Shuri had rounded up all her warriors. She had dressed up in her full attire for battle, with her bow in hand and arrows tied to her back as they waited at strategic areas near the canal. She had earlier requested that they should take the king to a safe area separate from the palace, but he refused and chose to stay in the room where Obinna was.

The sorcerer was in that room with them too.

"There is an eerie silence in here," the king said to his

sorcerer.

He was afraid. He jumped when he heard a sound that seemed to be coming from outside the room. It was the parrot Udele, saying "Prophecy, prophecy," but they could not see where she perched.

The drunkard picked up an object and intended to run outside with it, find and hurt the bird, but the sorcerer held his hands and said:

"No, it is how it was meant to be."

The Shuri at the canal heard the horses as they emerged, and they stood their ground. It was the warriors from Tangandoom but, much to their surprise, only three warriors were there. The executioner was not amongst them, so the Shuri wondered if it was all a distraction. They stopped at the canal as their horses neighed and raised their hooves high up in the air. One of the warriors from Tangandoom got off his horse holding a bag which had something it concealed. He held it up at the Shuri who was nearby. When she began to approach, the warrior threw the bag on the ground, got back on his horse with his men and yelled back at her:

"This is my executioner's gift to you! Give it to the one that bears the flute; it will be your final warning."

And they rode off on their horses.

The Shuri picked up the bag in a hurry, opened it and looked inside as her warriors looked on. What she saw inside the bag made her stomach rumble. She fell backwards in shock and rolled over.

"No, no, no!" she cried as her warriors gathered to find out what the men had dropped off. They looked inside and grimaced when they saw its contents too. It was an amputated human hand that they had severed from the wrist.

The executioner had cut off Adaure's right hand at Tangandoom and sent it to them as a warning for what is yet to come if they refused to comply. Her warriors were not sure who the hand belonged to, but the Shuri knew Obinna's story. She knew they were Adaure's.

She ran off with the bag, headed towards the pedestal where Obinna lay as her warriors ran after her. She would trip, fall and roll over but pick herself up again and continue running.

Clouds began to gather in the skies, and it looked as though a terrible storm was on its way, but she kept running. The winds became stronger as she arrived at the door of the room where Obinna lay. She was totally out of breath by the time she got there.

The king, the sorcerer, Igwekala and the drunkard all turned around as she hopelessly walked over to Obinna, brought out Adaure's severed hand from the bag and threw it at Obinna's chest.

"I am sorry; this is your Adaure; you might as well sleep forever now; they will kill her eventually."

*

Some things that happen sometimes are better if they are left alone and not thought through. After all, what does the mind know? It understands self-preservation and how to add splendour, joy and meaning to our existence. Sometimes it ponders over love, hate and would often wonder why all that is born must have to die.

But when the mind gives up and shuts down is when magic comes alive; it is when it lends its helping hand to those who believe.

Magic is the air we breathe, the sounds we hear, and yes; the things that we feel.

Adaure's severed hand rolled down Obinna's chest and touched his hand, and he felt it.

And the oja around his waist came to life. It heated up and glowed so brightly that nobody in the room could look at it. Obinna's body became hot as the bright ray of light shone from the oja through his hands, to his head and down to his feet. The energy from the flute woke him up as he jumped up from the pedestal and the ray of light formed a halo around him.

Udele, the parrot, was heard as she let out a loud squawk, flew into the room and slumped on the ground, flapping its feathers and wriggling as though it was hurt.

He looked down, picked up the parrot by its legs as well as Adaure's hand and as he placed both in the bag, he screamed,

"Warriors whom destiny has chosen, run with me now towards Tangandoom and do not look back!"

They did run with him. Igwekala and the drunkard; the Shuri, the sorcerer, even the king. But they were not alone; Earth, wind, fire and water ran with them.

The hills that stood in their way moved aside, and rivers held their feet up as they sped across the surface of waters and lands.

Thunder, lightning, hurricanes and wildfires stood guard around them as they were lifted high up in the air and propelled further ahead.

That journey back to Tangandoom took them minutes even though the route should typically take days.

And when they arrived, Gandoom and his executioner and warrior's fate was already set.

They stood in line with their armoury and horses, mouths open and hands shaking as they saw Obinna descend from the skies with his oja in one hand and the bag in the other.

He descended and struck the earth on which the warriors stood with the oja.

And that was how it all ended.

The earth gave in, and there was a massive sinkhole where the king and his warriors stood.

It swallowed Gandoom, his executioner and all his warriors.

And they were never seen again.

*

The journey home was different. The oja had spared the rest of the villagers from Tangandoom. The sinkhole did not spread to where they were. They were all protected, including Adaure and her baby.

She and Obinna did not say much to themselves when they met face to face; their eyes told each other their story as they held hands while Obinna's daughter crept in the middle. She was already a year old and had just learnt how to walk.

Adaure spoke to him very briefly, "My love, so you found your magic."

"Yes, I found it because your magic found me first," he replied.

"What is her name?" Obinna asked Adaure.

"Her name is Ojanna; it means her father's oja," she

replied.

Obinna saw that someone appropriately tied Adaure's severed hand so she would not lose a lot of blood and he tried to have a look at it.

"The maidens tied it up; do not worry, I will be okay," she smiled and replied.

The Shuri informed them that they should take horses, food and water from Tangandoom for their journey, and the villagers were happy to give it to them.

The rest of his villagers from Umuzura who were still alive, including the elders, the maidens and the merchants, greeted Obinna when they saw him.

"Appoint yourselves a new king and get rid of the old wicked ways," he said to the villagers from Tangandoom as he waved them goodbye and left with the horses.

The drunkard married the Shuri on their way home, and Igwekala was the best man during the ceremony, which was overseen by the sorcerer and King Nuri.

King Nuri promised Obinna that he would send help over to Umuzura as soon as they got home to assist them in rebuilding their village from scratch and that he would continue to give the drunkard the proceeds from the palm wine trees in his gardens of pleasure.

The Shuri hugged his king and told him that she would visit him and the rest of her warriors often to make sure they were all okay.

The king and the sorcerer left them and headed back to Kanuri.

*

They got back to Umuzura, and the villagers wanted to honour and make Obinna their king, but he refused and asked them to appoint Igwekala instead.

"He will be our king in this village; the limping king." He praised him.

The celebrations had started as his villagers were singing and clapping with joy.

Obinna left them, walked further away but the drunkard and Igwekala followed closely behind. They were curious and wanted to see what he was doing. He had the bag in which Udele, the parrot, was held. Obinna gently picked the parrot up by its legs and brought it out as it spread and flapped its wings.

"Should we kill it now?" the drunkard asked him.

"No," Obinna said, "we have broken the curse; we do not have any need for prophecies anymore."

He told Igwekala that from then on, they would replace their Udunre festival with a festival he called "The Celebration of Life."

"The masquerades will be no more; rather, the maidens will dance in their place."

He caressed the bird's head, threw it high up in the air and released it.

"Go, Udele, go away and never return; we won," he urged the bird.

And the villagers clapped, cheered and laughed when they saw the parrot flying across the skies screaming, "We won, we won, we won!"

Obinna never blew that oja again. He left it alone and decided they would live their lives as usual.

"What next?" the drunkard and Igwekala asked him as

the celebrations continued.

"I have to go somewhere with my daughter, and I will be back shortly; there is something I must give her."

They watched as Obinna went to Adaure, carried his daughter on his bosom, took the oja out from the bag around his waist and headed towards that wooden bridge, built over the river that has its banks lined with coconut trees.

The End.